LITTLE WOLF

PAULINE WALTERS

Contents

For everyone who's ever felt small, out of place, or not enough:
you are, and always will be, enough.

Contents Warning

This story contains mature and potentially distressing themes, including violence, gore, blood, captivity, kidnapping, servitude, verbal and physical bullying within a pack dynamic, and torture both on and off page. It also includes mentions of sexual assault, rape, dubcon/noncon (light), sex work, sex slavery, suicide, homelessness, and the deaths of children. Elements of cheating (not between the main characters), body mutilation (on page), and genital mutilation (mention) are also present.

Even if those are not too strong or detailed, they're still present. Please take care of yourself.

Acknowledgements

I have to give a big thank you to my PA, Emma. Because if I don't, she'll come at me with her whip and I'd rather not risk it. (Though between us... I don't always mind a good whip session.

So yes, thank you, Emma.

Love you!

But also, big thanks and cuddles to my Street Team, who've been supporting my ass these last few months—and who, whenever I ask *"is this too much?"* always answer, *"nah, it's fine."*

CHAPTER I

I RACE THROUGH THE forest, the wind on my face, as if my entire body and soul were made for this. The earth is soft beneath me. It rained yesterday, and the mud is sticking to my paws, but I don't care. A fallen trunk blocks the path ahead, and without hesitation, I gather my speed and launch myself into the air, my back legs kicking until I land in a splash of thick mud. My wolf squeals with excitement inside of me.

I can't catch a bunny, but at least I can run. The thought creeps into my mind, uninvited but familiar. It's the full moon tonight, and once again, my pack has made fun of me for being the worst huntress of them all.

I've tried—really tried—to hunt, to catch anything that moves out here. Speed isn't my problem. It's everything else. Instead of failing in front of them again, I run to my favourite place deep in the forest, far away from the rest of the pack.

I know Kyle doesn't care anymore—he's too busy sniffing Alisha's furry butt.

As an infant, I was left on the side of the road, with nothing but a dirty diaper. I spent my life moving from average foster families to worse ones, until one day the wolf-shift happened, and I had to run away. When I found other werewolves, I thought I'd finally found my place—my family. But wow, was I wrong. Kyle, our Alpha, used to be the kindest man. Or at least I thought he was. Tall, dark, and handsome. You see the type? He cared for me and said my wolf's small size was cute. Not anymore. Now I get eye rolls and sighs every time I mess something up, which happens every full moon, without fail. Instead of being with them, I'm always alone. At the mansion or here in the woods. I just don't want to hear any more about how I'm a failure of a wolf.

Those bitter thoughts almost ruin my enjoyment, but I finally reach my destination—my peaceful oasis. The falls are beautiful, gigantic, loud, and wild. The water crashing below drowns out even your own thoughts. There's a hidden path behind the waterfalls, leading to a small cave where I love to hide when it rains too much for my taste.

My wolf and I, we don't like to get wet. This is the perfect place to nap instead of chasing dumb bunnies.

I trot to the edge of the pool and lean over, looking at my reflection. My wolf is so pretty—at least I think so. My fur is pure white, my eyes ice-blue, and my body barely matches the size of an average wolf. Nothing like the monster-wolves in my pack, three times my size. No wonder they make fun of me. I look like a pup even though I'm a grown-ass woman. I tried to joke with Kyle that 'size doesn't matter,' but he was not impressed with my sense of humour.

My ears flick as muffled screams echo through the forest. It's time. Shifting is always painful—bones breaking, limbs stretching, skin folding over itself. It's nasty.

But not for me.

Silver sparkles float around me, soft and bright, and the magic stirs in my veins. I let it wash over me, warm and familiar, shifting me into my human shape without a drop of pain.

I give my back a stretch and sigh, staring down at the water. I can't hear the screams anymore—human ears aren't as sharp—but I know they're still echoing through the woods as the others fight their way back to their human forms. The sun is rising.

The pool below me shifts colors, soft pink and purple, bleeding into the water with the first light of day. A tear slips down my cheek, and I wipe it away with muddy and angry fingers.

They don't know I can shift this easily. I've kept it hidden for so long that it feels like a weight I carry every day. I wanted to tell Kyle once upon a time. He gave me so much attention, promised to protect me, and made me feel seen. I was going to tell him. I'm glad I didn't. Now that I know him, I know what he would've done. He would've kicked me out, thrown me out of the only home I've ever had.

"They must never know," I whisper to my reflection, then stand and turn away, heading back toward the new day.

CHAPTER 2

ONE DOESN'T NEED TO be particularly sharp to realize I don't belong. I had known it from the first full moon with Kyle's pack. The whines, the groans, the way they all complained about the pain of shifting and the tiredness that came with it the following day—it had confused me. Why were they so afraid, so *hateful*, of something that, for me, came so easily? So peacefully? I kept quiet. I didn't want to draw attention and brag.

When I heard their screams that night, I knew something was up with me. Their yelps, begging for it to stop, resonated in my ears, sending waves of cold shivers through my body. So, I hid, using the excuse of being too shy to shift in front of them. It wasn't entirely a lie. I am not exactly comfortable showing off my body in front of a group of strangers, even though were-wolves seem not to mind a bit. The truth was something else. If they knew I could shift without pain, it would just confirm to them that I'm different, and I just wanted to belong. But now? It's too late to tell them. They'd hate me for it.

Well... they already kind of hate me. Or at least, they act like I don't exist. I tried so hard to fit in, to be one of them. After a few weeks, most of them stopped pretending to care, as if they could sense something was wrong with me, for something I didn't even understand myself.

And Kyle... even he stopped trying. I thought he'd hold on longer; that, being the Alpha and my boyfriend, he'd keep pulling me in, helping me to make my space, to be accepted. That was literally his job. When I think about the way he used to look at me—those intense eyes filled with adoration and pride—there's a sharp ache in my chest. Now his gaze skims past me, landing on everything and on everyone but me. The less I give him, the more he drifts away.

Lesson learned: do not get all touchy-touchy with your Alpha.

Not that I didn't try. I wanted to give myself to him, but every time he touched me, it felt... off. Gloria, one of the more brash pack-mates, would call it 'meh,' and she would not be wrong. Everything felt 'meh' between Kyle and me, especially in the bedroom. Foreplay was so awkward, unsatisfying, and borderline abusive. I never let it go further. And Kyle, at first, said he understood, said he could be patient.

Patient? I scoff at the memory as I descend the stairs of the massive three-story mansion the pack calls home. Patient, my ass. He'd pushed and pouted, whining about how we needed to 'take the next step' in our relationship. *"Men have needs, Mina."* Yeah? Well, I have needs too, and I'm not being an ass about it.

I always had an excuse. I always found a way to dodge the inevitable. I wasn't ready, and I'm still not ready, especially not with this kind of attitude from him. So here I am: a weak, useless wolf, still a virgin, holding on to the flimsy threads of a relationship I am not even sure I want anymore. Maybe I am reading too many romance books. Those book boyfriends have just raised my expectations, I guess.

It's more than that. Lately, Kyle has been... distant. Distracted. And I am not the only one who noticed. The little voice in my head is screaming that it has something to do with Alisha—the gorgeous, blonde bombshell who has never hidden her interest in Kyle.

"Kyle wouldn't do that," I told myself and my wolf over and over during the past few weeks.

He laughed when I confronted him about it some time ago, swearing his worries were only pack business. Indeed, there have been endless meetings about the potential regrouping of packs and an eventual confrontation with vampires. Maybe he was telling the truth, but I have a sixth sense about things like this, and my extra sense is screaming that I'm getting screwed.

As I reach the kitchen, I stop in the doorway. The delicious scent of bacon floats through the air, and I stare at a small group of wolves already gathered at the long wooden table. Gloria sits at the head, her feet up on the table, tearing into a piece of toast. Across from her, Alisha is laughing—so loudly, so carefree. Of course, she is here. She is always here. I force myself to look away, trying to focus on something else. Unfortunately, my brain decides to focus on the conversation and the way it stopped the second I stepped inside.

"Morning, Mina," Gloria says, not bothering to look up. Her tone was flat, as if being polite is the strict minimum she can do when I'm concerned. We never got along that much.

"Morning," I mumble, sliding past her toward the counter, where the coffee pot still has a few drops left. I can feel their eyes on me, lingering for just a second too long. Do I need to mention that I am not that great with groups of people?

"Sleep well?" Alisha asks. I think her voice is laced with some fake sweetness, but maybe I'm just paranoid.

I glance over my shoulder. "Fine, thanks."

I probably slept better than her, seeing how well my body is reacting to my shift. I can see with the way they sit on their chairs that they're hurting today.

She says nothing after that, but the way she smirks as I pour my coffee makes my skin crawl. I am not stupid. I can see how Kyle's eyes watch her sometimes. He used to look at me the same way.

I hear whispers behind me. Quiet, but not quiet enough. I hear the word 'hunt,' and I know they are talking about me. About how weak I am. How I don't belong here. They used to tolerate me because of Kyle, because I could have been the next Luna. But now? Now, I am not even sure if I am still his girlfriend, which, to be honest, would not disturb me that much; I'm kind of done with the guy. If he wants to go with Alisha or another, maybe it would be for the best?

I sip my coffee, enjoying the rough taste on my tongue, and lean against the counter, trying to ignore the ache in my chest. Kyle walks in, his hair slightly mussed like it always is, his shirt unbuttoned halfway down his chest. He looks distracted, which is the norm these days.

"Hey," I mutter, hoping to get some kind of acknowledgement.

He nods in my direction, barely looking at me as he grabs a piece of toast from the counter. "Morning, Mina."

That's it. No kisses. No smile. Just... morning. He treats me like I am any other member of the pack, not his girlfriend, not someone he is supposed to care about. I stare at him, waiting for something more, but he sits down next to Alisha without a second glance in my direction. It's getting worse after each full moon now. This is just confirming what I thought I knew.

A knot forms in my stomach. Of course, he'd sit next to her. The voice in my head is practically shouting now, reminding me of all the times he'd dismissed my concerns about her. 'It's just pack business, Mina. You're overreacting.' That's what he says, but I am not overreacting. I know.

Freaking liar, little piece of shit. If you're going to dump me, at least do it before getting your dick wet with another woman.

I push away from the counter, my appetite gone, and go to the back door. I need air. As I step outside, the crisp morning breeze hits my face. For a moment, I let myself forget, enjoying this. I wish I could run into the forest, maybe sleep in there on the soft, lush moss at my falls. And ignore all of those idiots. Who cares, after all, if I can't catch a damn bunny? It's not like there's no grocery store just fifteen minutes away. They're acting as if we are living during a zombie apocalypse, and we all need to be good hunters, but there's literally Uber Eats now, delivering to our house.

I sigh. I know I can't ignore this situation forever, especially the way it makes me feel. Something is happening, and deep down, I know it is only going to get worse.

Later that day, when the afternoon sun filters through the windows, casting long shadows across the walls, something weird happens. I want to talk to Kyle, clear the air between us, and maybe get him to dump me so I can go on with my life. I was not planning to sneak up on him, but here he is, with his back turned to me. The muscles in his shoulders stretch out the too-small T-shirt he always wears. Yes, Kyle is one of those guys. The guys who like to wear tiny T-shirts to show off their muscles. It is perfectly ridiculous, if you ask my opinion, but then fashion isn't really my thing. I practically live in dresses, most of them second-hand from the village shop. Don't start me on Kyle's thoughts about me wearing something old and not worth hundreds of dollars. You would think werewolves were pretty chill. Well, spoiler alert: they're not.

This isn't about the clothes. No, this is about the way he is bending down slightly... over her.

Alisha.

Alisha and her bouncy, curly, perfect freaking chevelure framing her face as she gazes up at him, those doe eyes wide and innocent. I want to hate her, I really do, but she'd never been outright mean to me. Well, aside from the whole 'batting my long eyelashes in front of your boyfriend' stuff.

They are whispering, their voices too low for me to make out the words, but it doesn't matter; I'm not that dumb. I see the way they look at each other, the kind of look only lovers should exchange. My heart clenches painfully in my chest. This... this is it. The thing I have been dreading. The thing I have refused to confront, even though, if I'm being honest, it was right under my nose for a little while.

Before I can process the heartbreak sinking in, my eyes catch on something else—something strange. Kyle is holding a leather-bound book, old and worn. He points out a passage to Alisha, whispering. I don't have time to wonder what all of this is about before Alisha's gaze catches mine. The moment she spots me, her expression shifts through a variety of feelings. From innocent and seductive, to a slight panic, to smug.

Kyle turns, his expression unreadable; you would almost think he hasn't done anything bad at all. For a brief second, something flickers in his dark eyes. Guilt? Regret? Or maybe I am just imagining it.

"Mina," he says, his voice flat. "What do you want?"

What do I want? I scoff. Is he serious? I am not ready to confront the elephant in the room. Not yet. My eyes drift back to the book.

"What's the book?" I ask, more curious than I want to admit. Anything to avoid the truth glaring back at me.

Kyle and Alisha exchange a quick glance, and he hands the weird, smelly book to her. Yes, it is smelly: musty old leather, something faintly rotten beneath. Given how dull my sense of smell is compared to the others, this thing has to stink.

"Nothing for you to worry about," Kyle replies, his tone dismissive. "It's Alpha business. For the regrouping."

"She's not an Alpha," I dare to say, pointing at the woman with my chin, not wanting to unclench my arms, holding as tightly as I can, my nails digging into my skin.

Kyle licks his lips. His attention is fixed on some imaginary point on the floor—his way of showing he is going to lie. Oh, I know him by heart now. I glance at Alisha, whose lips curl into a sexy smirk that makes me want to punch her. Not that punching her would be a great idea; she is the strongest of the females in here, and she's feral!

"You could at least wear your balls and tell me the truth, Kyle," I say dryly, my voice sharper than I intended. "You know, instead of leaving me to be the last idiot in this house to figure it out."

Kyle steps closer, his Alpha presence pressing down on me like a weight. He loves doing this—trying to use his power to intimidate me, to make me feel small. Too bad it never works. That is the real problem between us. I wouldn't break beneath him. He grunts.

I am a failed werewolf if I cannot feel my own Alpha's presence.

"Do not talk to me that way, Mina." His voice is low, dangerous, the rumble in it showing that he's still trying to assert his dominance over me. He turns to Alisha, who is still holding the book against her chest like it is some sacred relic. He reaches for her hand, and that small gesture is enough to tear a hole in my heart. "Alisha is going to be my Luna. I've talked to the other Alphas, who are joining us soon, and they agree she's the best fit."

There it is. The truth I have been avoiding. The best fit.

I swallow the lump forming in my throat, trying to ignore the stabbing pain in my chest. Knowing what was coming does not make it easier. "Okay, first of all, we haven't decided yet about this regrouping of yours. I asked a few ancients, and they all mentioned that having so many wolves—Alphas—under one roof was insanity, unnatural."

Kyle's jaw tightens. "And that's why all their previous packs are gone, wiped out by the vampires. We can't afford to be weak, Mina." He looks at me from head to toe, while I catch a glimpse of a smirk on Alisha's face. I know exactly what he is implying.

My blood boils. "The vote isn't done yet."

"It will be. Please don't make stuff complicated. It's happening, Mina. All of it. You should have been..." He trails off, searching for the right word.

"Sluttier?" I help him, the word tasting bitter on my tongue.

He scoffs, while Alisha lets out a giggle, her lips twitching in amusement.

"Whatever you want to believe," he mutters.

And then they leave. *They leave!* Just like that. They walk away, leaving me standing there, my heart shattered and my mind spinning. Are we done with this conversation? Did they seriously walk away from me like I was nothing?

I stand there for a long moment, staring after them, the weight of everything crashing down on me. My chest tightens, the sharp pain of betrayal cutting deeper than I thought it could.

He's really gone.

I am not just losing my boyfriend, which is kind of okay, I guess. I am losing my place in the pack. My future. Everything I thought I had.

And I'm the only one who's going to care about it.

CHAPTER 3

"**F**UCKING VAMPIRES HAVE A king now."

There it is. The official confirmation of what our pack has feared for moons. Our mortal enemies—according to Kyle—have a king. According to the Ancients of our pack, he is not to be messed with.

If anyone had bothered to ask me, I would have told them that no vampires should be messed with. But nobody asked. Nobody asked because I am the ex-Luna, the dumped woman who is no longer important, no longer worth considering.

Not gonna lie, I am thankful the attention has shifted from my disgrace to this looming vampire threat. My status in the pack has never been great, but now it is practically non-existent. To make it worse, I have to endure watching Kyle and Alisha play their little game of 'perfect couple' every chance they get, their hands sneaking into places that should be kept in the bedroom.

The pack is on edge. I can feel it in every tense body around me, in the whispered conversations, and in the overall grumpy mood in the house.

I get it, I do. Vampires are stronger, faster, and immortal—and most importantly, they don't have to go through the worst pain of their life every freaking month on the calendar. Sure, we wolves are fast and strong—others, not me—but nothing compared to what vampires can do. And immortality? Forget it. We have one advantage, and it isn't even in our favor right now: we can reproduce easily. Vampires, on the other hand, are doomed in that department—from what I heard, only the ancient ones can create new vampires.

I asked Kyle about it once, back when things were good between us, and he brushed me off, saying it wasn't my business. I also wanted to ask if they liked garlic or not, but felt it was probably not the right time.

I pout when I think about the conversation. I was more curious about vampires than I should have been, and he was upset I would take any interest in someone other than him. Maybe I should start paying attention to red flags. I also should borrow this book about narcissistic perverts that I saw at the library.

I shift against the wall I picked to hide behind, glancing around the packed room. There are no seats left; the room is filled with members from all the various packs that have agreed to come. I haven't seen this many pack members gathered in one place before. We are supposed to vote today on the damn regrouping. Having more people in the house who ignore me does not seem like the best idea in the world, but who knows? I might make new friends.

I force myself not to stare too long at the four other alphas standing beside Kyle. They are the textbook definition of an alpha male—muscular, arrogant, and cruel. I shiver at the realization, clenching my arms tighter around my waist. These are not men who are going to make my life easier. I can feel it. They are all about strength and power.

Talks have been going on for what seems like hours, but really, it hasn't. The Alphas are listing all the reasons for the regrouping—strength in numbers, better protection, and unity in the face of the vampire threat. Funnily enough, all pros, no cons. It feels like the decision has already been made, and we are all just here to approve their plans.

A member from a pack that has recently been attacked by a nearby vampire nest gives a detailed account of the slaughter. They have lost dozens of members, including children. At the mention of rape, my stomach turns. The thought of those poor kids, those women... I get it, but I don't think we should judge an entire species based on what a few of them did. After all, if vampires wanted to slaughter werewolves, we would have been gone for hundreds of years. I understand why we'd be safer in a regrouping, but this seems so... unhealthy. A little society stuck in a few houses, spread among some hectares of fields. And so many Alphas? How can that go right? With their oversized egos?

Our pack already has the largest number and domain, with much space to live our lives hidden from the neighbors' townships and lots of space for new homes to be built. It isn't space I am worried about. It is the power dynamics. Too many alphas in one place—it feels like a ticking time bomb.

The vote is happening, and I still have this feeling that something bad is coming.

Kyle's voice cuts through the murmurs, his fists resting on his hips as he surveys the room, stopping on Alisha, who gives him an encouraging smile. Her hands are clasped together, the perfect posture of a first lady.

"You've all heard our reasoning," Kyle says. "We believe this is the best way to stop this new king. Who votes for the regrouping?"

I hold back a sigh as I witness hands shoot up around me, all voting in favor of what I think is a terrible idea. I am not a follower, so I keep my head and my hands down. Kyle doesn't need my vote. He has more than enough support.

When the silence is starting to be disturbing, I raise my head, unsure of what I will find.

When I meet Kyle's gaze, my breath catches. *Oopsie.* His eyes are black, as dark as a storm, and they are locked on me. Fury radiates from him, thick and suffocating. I can feel the tremor in his skin, his Alpha power attempting to assert itself over me.

Still not working, buddy.

Gloria, sitting next to me, jabs her elbow into my ribs, making me wince. "Raise your fucking hand," she hisses, her voice barely audible.

I can hear a slight panic in her voice.

I scoff and cross my arms over my chest. As if that will protect me from the five furious alphas staring me down. Even Alisha looks nervous, her eyes darting between me and Kyle, silently begging me to fall in line.

Fine. I smirk and raise my hand in a slow, exaggerated motion, making sure my expression shows exactly how little I approve. Not that it matters. I spot the disgust on Marco's face, one of the Alphas, and can't help but swallow. Am I going to regret this? I blame my wolf. She's crazy sometimes.

"Good," Kyle says, his voice sharp, never breaking eye contact with me. "Now that it's decided, we move on to the second topic of this meeting."

Second topic? My shoulders straighten as I notice the curious glances being cast my way, while others pointedly avoid looking at me altogether.

That's not good.

"Regrouping calls for a new order," Marco says as he steps forward, taking over from Kyle.

My stomach twists. I shift uncomfortably, knowing full well what's coming. This is it. My official destitution as Luna. Saying it aloud in front of close to hundreds of wolves was really unnecessary; I'm sure they all got the memo.

"We want to return to the traditions of the older packs," Marco continues, his voice cold and cutting, "where a member of this family who doesn't pull their weight faces consequences."

Okay... maybe it's not about the Luna thing?

When Marco's icy gaze locks on me, I know better. It is about me.

"Mina," he says, his tone hard, "we, Alphas of the Pack, have decided to demote you. You will now be the first Omega of this new family. Showing what happens when one does not suit the pack."

The words hit me like a punch to the gut. I can't believe what I'm hearing.

"What the fuck?" I explode, my voice ringing out across the room, fueled by the fury roaring inside me. I hope it sounds strong and defiant, but I feel the tremors in my voice giving me away.

"Watch your mouth when you talk to one of us!" Marco yells, startling me. I can feel his furor. I can feel his intense vibrations. He is trying to use his Alpha sense on me. Maybe Kyle should have told him I'm broken.

Kyle steps forward, placing a hand on Marco's shoulder, turning his attention to me. I search his face, desperately hoping for a flicker of remorse or regret, some sign he still cares.

There's nothing. His eyes are cold.

"You'll be free to leave the pack in six months if you wish," Kyle says, as if he is doing me a favor.

I scoff, the sound dripping with disbelief. "Fuck that. I'm leaving now. I'm not a slave." I whirl toward the other pack members, their faces a mixture of pity and shame, most of them still avoiding my eyes. "You should be ashamed of what they're doing! When I'm gone, do you think they'll stop? Who's next in line to be their Omega? If you're not an Alpha, or a man, do you think you're safe?"

"*Enough*, Mina!" Kyle's voice cuts through the air as he strides toward me. His Alpha power presses down like a weight on my chest, but it's still not enough to break me. "Six months to pay for what the pack has paid for you those last six months. It's a common practice with Omegas. You reimburse us, then if you want to leave the pack, good riddance."

"If I knew that every single bite I took from our daily bunnies was going to lead me to that, I would have gone and bought myself some fucking pizza at the shop."

"Well, you can still do that to avoid getting your reimbursement to take longer," retorts Kyle, a cruel smirk on his once handsome face. The asshole is enjoying this situation way too much.

I heard once about the whole Omega bullshit system. As the lowest of the low, you have to work your ass off to do all the shitty jobs around the house, but you also have to pay for your food and rent in any way you can. Either by taking on more jobs or just starving, I guess. I have very little cash left, so I'm not gonna last long with this. I'd better get good at catching bunnies really fast.

Lost in my thoughts, I almost miss what's happening. Marco moves toward the fire in the living room, bending over the flames. When I see the pity-filled looks in the eyes of the pack members around me, it hits me.

The marking. *Fuck*. I forgot about the marking.

My heart drops into my stomach. Marco straightens up, holding the firebrand in his hand, the glowing red Omega symbol at the tip searing into my vision.

"No!" I protest, but two of my lovely pack-mates are already holding me, arms in my back, held in an iron clench. Panic surges through me as I struggle, but their grip is too strong. I'm thrown to the ground, still fighting, but it's pointless. My weakness is right here for everyone to witness, but I will not give them the pleasure of begging.

My wolf is howling inside me, crying and begging, filled with rage and pain. We need to run. We need to fight. It's no use. There's nowhere to go. Nowhere to hide. I want to tell her I'm sorry. I wish I could comfort her, tell her this isn't our fault. The truth is, I failed us both. *I can't, little wolf, I'm sorry.*

And then it happens.

The firebrand touches my skin, and the pain explodes through my body. A scream tears from my throat, primal and raw. It's not just the pain of the burn; it's the shame. The humiliation. I can hear the sickening sizzle of my flesh, and the smell hits me like a punch in the face. My right shoulder feels like it's on fire, the brand etching deep into my skin, marking me as an Omega for everyone to see. I know they will soon place some moonbane to stop me from healing, keeping this mark forever.

My mind is spinning. I want to claw at the mark, tear it from my skin, and rip it away. All I can do is lie there, panting, my body trembling in the soaring pain.

I lie on the floor, defeated, as the room comes back into focus. The faces of my pack-mates are a blur of horror and indifference. No one comes to help me. No one even moves.

I've been branded. Stripped of my dignity.

The worst part? The burn is nothing compared to the ache in my chest.

I have become the Omega.

CHAPTER 4

TURNS OUT WHEN YOU'RE demoted to Omega, life *does* get worse.

I swear I will never complain again about my life from before.

I mean, I already had no friends, and now I have to pay for the roof over my head. The food I eat? Also on the tab. I was fine with the isolation before, but I had Kyle. Or at least I had him at the start of our relationship. Now? He treats me like I'm dirt, like I'm an old minty chewing gum stuck to his shoe. Which, according to the new rules, I am. The lowest of the low.

Is being an Omega just a fancy term for being a modern slave? Oh, absolutely. Kyle even had the nerve to tell me I should be *grateful*—in the older days, I'd be chained to the wall at night, used as a toy for whichever men wanted me. Yuck. I'm at least glad this is not on the menu. How does he even know that much about the older days? I bet you he doesn't, but he sure isn't showing any kind of feeling. He was not that much of a show-off before, to be honest, but now... oh man, now...

I sigh while packing away the last clean dishes, trying my best not to drop one. If I do, it'll go straight into my debt.

Dishes, laundry, and babysitting. *All* of it is on me now. Funny enough, looking after the children is the only part of this whole mess I don't mind. I do mind when they ask questions about why I'm being treated differently. Children are smart; you can't hide the whole servant thing going on. What am I supposed to tell them? I feel bad for them growing up in this, thinking maybe one day this will be their turn if they are not good enough.

I also don't have the right to eat with the pack. I eat after; I eat the leftovers. My debt increases with every bite I take. I have never been a big eater, so I try to take as little as I can, stealing some stuff here and there. The forest is my friend. Those idiots can hunt all the rabbits they want. I know where to find berries and leaves to survive, and when I am really desperate, I run to the township and use whatever I can find in those honesty boxes, where the locals drop food surplus. *Bless them!*

At first, my old pack-mates were, for the most part, throwing me looks of pity. Some gave me soft smiles and promised it would get better. I could almost believe them. I think they almost believed it too, but not anymore. The Alphas made sure to stop the kindness right away, growling at anyone who dared to show me a shred of sympathy. Now, they don't even meet my eyes. This whole mess? Apparently, it's in their Bible; that's what I call the ugly, smelly book they are always gathering around.

I still ask myself every day how the hell I ended up here. Then I remember—*Kyle*. It always comes back to him. I trusted him. I cared for him. I can't say I loved him because love didn't have time to grow. Now, look at me—his discarded toy.

Red flag, Mina, the freaking red flags. They were right there.

Now that all the packs have grouped, it's chaos. This place has become a busy hive. At first, it made things a little better. I was just one small bee, lost in the crowd. Our Alphas decided I would mostly serve my pack and Alphas if they needed, but others could do without me. Rumor has it they're looking for an Omega from each of the newly joined packs, which is also one of the reasons people stopped showing they cared for me. I don't blame them. Five Omegas in total. Imagine that—building an entire system of servitude. You would think that mortal history should have taught them one or two things, right?

I stole some paper and a fancy pen from Kyle's office. The pen itself is probably worth a hundred dollars, so I'm not planning on getting this added to my debt. With those tools, I keep track of my debt, which keeps accumulating day after day, despite my hard work. Six months, they said, and I could leave. Every meal, every second spent under this roof, adds to the pile. The more I work, the bigger the debt gets, despite me not touching the food in the house—unless I steal it.

I am to the point of considering going for a sleep in the forest. I don't fear the trees; I don't fear the owls singing at me, and summer is coming now. I might even be fine without my fur. If they want to play this game, I can play better. It's either this or I'm running away at the next full moon in a few days. I wanted to be honest and pay my debt till the last cent, but... do they really deserve it? While they are all busy in the forest breaking their bones, I could just come back to the mansion and steal a car. Fuck honesty. Reality slaps me in the face. *Where* am I supposed to go? With no money, no plan? And an army of grumpy werewolves on my back?

I hold back a sigh as I head to the laundry room. A few days ago, I was warned that my poor, sensitive pack-mates don't appreciate hearing me complain or sigh too much. Apparently, it disturbs their peace. Still, I bite my tongue and focus on my next Omega duty.

Laundry, eww.

I hate laundry. Out of all my chores, it's the one I loathe the most. Touching the dirty clothes worn by smelly, sweaty, and—let's be honest—horny wolves? *Yuck.* I'm bad at it, which doesn't help. It's also a thing to suck at laundry. I thought for a little while, maybe one week or so, that if I was bad enough at it, they would stop entrusting me with it. That didn't work out *at all* the way I planned, and I was punished for it with no food for two days. I got through thanks to the woods.

So now, I'm trying—not that hard, let's not push it, but I'm trying. I fold the clothes, one by one, trying not to linger too long on the fine fabrics of Alisha's and the other women's clothes. Alisha's ones, especially, are so soft, delicate, and expensive. I can't help but touch them a little longer than I should, running my fingers over the luxurious material. They make me feel small, like I don't belong anywhere near something so nice. Not with the way my life is now. For a brief moment, I imagine myself wearing something so elegant, something that *wasn't* handed down or torn. A girl can only love thrift stores so much.

What would a vampire queen wear? I imagine a red and black dress with so many laces you could almost see through it. Cliché, I know, but I truly wonder how vampires actually dress. *Vampires.* The thought always creeps in. More importantly, do they wear capes?

Voices filter in from the game room next door, pulling me from my daydreams. My ears perk up when I catch the word 'vampires.'

"Vampires are getting close. Jo from Helensville told me so." I recognize the raspy voice—it's Mark, one of the new pack members.

Right, those damn vampires, the ones who I can technically blame for some of my troubles. If they were not 'vampiring' around, going all bitey and stuff, maybe the Alphas would not care about having only strong hunters and fighters in their pack.

"Those damn bloodsuckers! I heard the king's a pure asshole, slaughtering everything in his way—especially wolves." That's Gloria. Gloria, who has been trying quite hard to find a boyfriend among the new packs that have joined. Too bad for her, they are all enjoying her wide-open legs, but not that much of her conversation.

"Yeah, well, he's gonna have a surprise when he comes by here. We got the numbers, and we're the only ones that can kill those MF."

Only on a full moon, though, I want to add, snickering in my folded shirt. Vampires are stronger than us; it's a fact. Can we kill them when we are wolves? Yep, we can, or so I heard. But when we are not on four legs, we are nowhere close to the speed or the strength, or even our teeth might not pierce their skin. What do I know? I'm just an Omega. I doubt anyone's going to ask for my input on fighting tactics.

They can only attack at night, so we may have a slight advantage during the day. Do they really think vampires have survived centuries without planning for that? There's no way they don't have some sort of protection while they sleep. I bet their king has even more tricks up his sleeve. I promise to add this to my list of questions about vampires: do they sleep in a coffin?

I've always been fascinated by vampires—what makes them... them? How were they born? Even the Ancients in our pack don't exactly have any answers to this.

My fingers brush against one of Alisha's satin dresses, and I lose myself in the sensation. It's soft, cool, perfect—so unlike the basic ones I like to wear. My most prized possession is actually a green velvet dress that I found at the closest thrift store—oh, surprising—with a square cleavage that has the tendency to attract all the wolves. I haven't worn it in a while; avoiding looks and attention is better for now. While I caress Alisha's soft, elegant dress, I imagine what it would feel like to wear something like this without worrying about dropping food on it, like I often do.

A loud laugh from the game room pulls me back to reality, and I shake my head. Right. That's not gonna happen anytime soon, especially if I damage more clothes.

As I carefully place the dress down, the door creaks open, and guess who sneaks in? Leaning casually against the frame, her thin lips curled into a smirk, it's Madame Luna herself—Alisha. She has a smile on her face; the woman hasn't even thrown a glance at me since I became an Omega. Let's be honest, she didn't care much before that either. She was too busy screwing my boyfriend.

I glance up at her, raising an eyebrow, bracing myself for whatever weird or irritating conversation is coming. I don't want to start this, not with her. She smiles and steps forward, closing the door smoothly behind her. Her shiny blond hair flies around her head like she's turning in a shampoo commercial, and I can't help but tidy one of my wild curls behind my ear.

"Can I give you some advice?" she asks. "Woman to woman?" Her teeth show, but her eyes don't change.

I click my tongue, fighting the urge to roll my eyes. *Great.* "Sure."

If she tells me which settings to use for my laundry, I swear I'll slam her head into the washing machine. If I can.

What comes is quite surprising and worse than ill-advice on laundry.

"In this new order, you're gonna need to open your legs."

I blink, staring at her like she grew sparkly horns on her head. "What the fuck?" I scoff, searching for some trace of a bad sense of humor on her face. Oh my god, she's serious.

"You're an Omega now, Mina." Her voice drops to a whisper, and she steps closer. "You *will* get fucked sooner or later, but if you're smart, you'll make it work for you."

I almost believe for one second that she actually cares, which makes me happier than it should.

"Kyle said I didn't have to do that..." Becoming the little whore of the house is last on my wish list. I'd rather have a hundred angry werewolves chasing me through the woods than this.

Alisha lets out a soft sigh, as if my ignorance disappoints her. "In the end, Kyle will follow the lead of the other Alphas, and they know more about the way this new order works. And... you're pretty." She has added this last sentence with regret. I can feel it, as if she didn't want to admit it. I should be glad the shampoo goddess is jealous of me, but I'm too busy panicking.

I slam my hand on the laundry machine, trying not to wince under the light pain. "I won't become a whore, Alisha. People won't stand for it. Also, that's rape."

She barely reacts. "I'm just trying to help. First of all, this would pay your debt faster, you know? Second, it's not considered rape if you're an Omega. And third, if you don't want to get passed around by every Alpha, and then by every male, play smarter, girl."

"What the hell do you mean by playing smarter?" I truly have no idea what her advice means, still holding back my retch at the 'it's not a rape if you're an omega' argument.

Alisha sighs, as if she is explaining to a prepubescent little sister how babies are made. She moves a tad closer and whispers, "If you don't want to get taken by every male, then attack first. Go for the strongest Alpha. Make him like you, make him desire you so much he won't let anyone put a finger on you. Boys are possessive. They don't like to share their toys if they can avoid it." After this quite matter-of-fact speech, she straightens up, crossing her arms over her chest. "That's what I did."

I glance at her. She's serious. Damn it. *Bitch.*

"I really don't like any of them, though," I mutter, the words slipping out without much thought. How could I even like them when they treat me like dirt? I'm done with the Alpha-hole business.

Alisha chuckles. "Yeah, I figured so. Sometimes you have to sacrifice; it's just for a few months, and I can tell you with the way they look at you, they all will be glad to be the first ones to fuck you. You're weak, but at least you're cute. You can make that work for you."

I shudder at the thought. The image of their hands on me, their eyes… *yuck*. I feel sick.

"Except Kyle, obviously," she says. "The deal is that I give you good advice, and in exchange, you aim for another alpha."

"*So* generous of you, Alisha." I scoff. Trust me, I do want to be with a man. Like most of my pack-mates, I am also quite horny—they don't need to know that—except that I seem to have better control over it. I wish to have some basic respect beforehand—the strict minimum.

"Just saying. Do what you want with it." With that, she turns on her heel, gliding out of the room and leaving me alone with the piles of dirty laundry and the sickening images of Alphas hovering over me, their breath heavy, their hands greedy.

Yuck.

Yuck.

Yuck.

The sun sets behind the hills, and I take a break from the bathroom cleaning to admire this time of day. I sigh. This might be the best thing about this disastrous day.

Alisha's 'advice' has been on my mind, and usually nausea reaches me as soon as I try to classify our Alphas from the worst to the best choice. I wince when my body betrays me, sending a wave of pain. My periods have unfortunately arrived, and I would be much better lying down. Periods for us also mean we are hornier than usual, which could become a problem.

"I can't do that," I mutter to myself. If I could not give myself to Kyle, who I thought loved me and I loved him, how am I supposed to be a talented enough actress to convince one of those Alpha-holes?

"Can't do what?"

I jump—*damn it!* How hard can it be to hear people sneaking behind me? I'm supposed to be a freaking wolf with a full set of instincts. I contract my jaw involuntarily when I spot Marco, one of the Alphas, the one who too gladly announced my demotion as an Omega. His smile is cold, and his body takes up the entire door frame, but his eyes are what trigger my internal alarm.

"Do you need the bathroom?" I ask, already activating myself to get my cleaning stuff out of the way.

This is when I make the mistake of bending down to catch my bucket. An overly warm body approaches behind me, pushing against my bottom.

Oh, nononononononono.

I straighten back up and turn on my heels, both hands pushing the firm body away from me. My push makes no difference.

"I need to go now," I say, trying to give my voice some strength.

"Do you?" Marco asks, his arm catching me at the waist, pulling me against him and holding me way too hard and too close.

"Yep. Yep, I do; lots of stuff to do still, Omega job and all." I chuckle, my laugh sounding so fake; I know it's not gonna help. See? That's what I meant by 'bad acting.'

"How about you act nice for once, and I'll make sure you don't have anything else to do today *and* tomorrow?"

So generous.

Really, he and Alisha could get into a competition of who is the most generous in this pack, and I would have trouble deciding the winner.

I am ready to reply with a straight no when his hand moves behind my neck, catching me in an iron claw, bending my head to the back. My wincing does not change a thing, and I panic, fearing what's coming.

"Get on your knees, Omega. We have waited enough. If you're good enough, I might keep you for my own tonight."

Yuck.

"No," I don't need to think anymore. I know what I want and don't want, and I don't want *that*. "This was not part of the deal," I add, weakness cracking through my voice.

Marco erupts in laughter. Asshole.

"Which deal? There's no deal; Omegas don't have a choice. Kyle has been too lenient with you. The only thing you gotta be good at is taking care of us. Literally."

My eyes fill with tears, and my mouth trembles, but I fight back. This asshole won't get me so easily. I push him back. He's barely moving, but now he's furious at me, which is not helping.

A savage scream erupts from my throat, furious and as loud as I possibly can. I know some other wolves will come and help, won't they? Come on, guys, a rape is happening in your house, where your families live.

My scream is shut off by a giant hand around my neck, squeezing the sound out of it. I can barely wince in my pain, so calling for help is not an option. Marco pushes me against the sink, hitting my back against the cold marble, and I already know a bruise is gonna be there tomorrow. I don't heal well compared to others.

I'm still trying to kick him, but the lack of oxygen and the panic settling inside of me are not helping, and when he violently turns me over and forces my back to bend down, I cry. My vision is blurry with tears, and my cheek presses against the sink. The lemongrass cleaner fills my pores. I feel his hands are active on my back, and my broken voice tries one more time to protest when my leggings are pulled down over my ass, offering myself to him.

"Shush, darling, it's gonna be fine. Can't stay a virgin all your life now, can you?" he whispers into my ear, bending over me. He lets out a low growl. "You're bleeding, but it'll do anyway."

I can only see stars flying around my vision. I wait for it. I wait for the pain and the shame, but it does not come.

Marco releases my neck, and I scramble onto the floor, staring at him. He is standing straight, his eyes over toward the door, hands in a fist, and then he turns to me. "Vampires. You may die a virgin after all."

CHAPTER 5

MARCO IS GONE BEFORE I have time to say something smart. I don't move. I can't. I can barely bring my breath back to its normal rhythm. Marco has left the room, leaving me like a vulgar slut he would have found in a nightclub. My pants cling to my thighs, twisted and halfway down. My tank top lost one of its shoulder straps, the fabric hanging sadly. I bring my hands to my throat as I realize how much it hurts; the simple act of swallowing burns. A sob almost escapes me, but I force it down. *Not now.* Even though all I want is to roll in a ball and cry.

My legs shake under me, and a shiver runs through my entire body. An ice-like feeling envelopes me as if it is the middle of winter and I have no fur to protect me. Fear. Not from the vampires downstairs, but from Marco. From all of them.

Then it starts. Screams, raw and panicked. Then comes the noise of furniture breaking down and the sound of bodies being thrown around.

I clutch the sink, my nails biting into the porcelain. I'm too wobbly. Maybe I should just close the door and hope for the best. I look toward the small window. I could jump through it and run. I can shift fast enough to land gracefully on my wolf's paws.

My pragmatic side takes over: vampires are faster, so what's the point? I don't have time to think much more about the right decision when a shadow grows in the doorframe and my heart fastens. This is it. At least I won't get abused by one of my Alphas, by someone who had sworn to protect all of us.

I choose death.

A tiny man stands in the entrance, staring at me. I can't really say he is 'staring down' because I mean it: he's tiny. His hair is almost as fiery as mine, and his eyes are red, bright with excitement. From what I hear, the color is typical for vampires.

I can't admire my first vampire for too long, though, because one detail makes me happier than it should. As I lower my eyes, I see Marco's neck held in a tight clutch in the vampire's hand. Passed out.

Wow.

If I were not trying to breathe without panicking, I would be laughing.

He is also being lifted slightly from the floor, the same way I would lift one of the stray kittens I sometimes find in the shed. Those vampires are stronger indeed. Fighting them back is a ridiculous idea.

The little vampire seems as surprised to see me, and I understand quickly why when his eyes go down to my unclothed crotch.

"For fuck's sake," I mutter. First time meeting a vampire, first time probably being killed, and it would be in such an outrageous position? Hell no. Not on my watch.

Tiny-Red smiles, and I can see his fangs while I pull my pants back up. His eyes are fixated on my neck.

"Come down," he says. "We are gathering all of you downstairs." He has one of the strongest accents I have ever heard, but I'm too bad with accents to determine where he is from. He stops and adds, "You smell *really* good."

I quickly readjust myself, making sure none of my blood dripped onto my pants, and I step forward. There's not much I can do with whatever is left of my outfit. Tiny-Red has left the bathroom before me, as if he didn't fear having this terrible, dangerous wolf threat behind his back. He probably doesn't.

We get down the stairs, and despite the fear still present, I enjoy the loud, rhythmic thud Marco's body makes on every stair. When I raise my head back up and focus on the scene below me, I freeze.

On a positive note, I guess the mansion is gonna be less busy now. I walk down the stairs one by one, taking my time to assess the damage. I count at least a dozen bodies of random wolves, some I know, some I don't. Only men were caught in the killing, it seems, and I'm curious to know if it's a lucky coincidence or purposeful. I won't complain about a few less males in this house.

Some of their bodies have been torn apart, so I have to count a few times before being sure of the disaster.

One of the vampires ushers me toward the ball-room—yes, our house has a ballroom. Don't ask me why.

Our Alphas are there.

Too bad they were not killed.

I have to hold back a disappointed pout. You would think that when you attack a werewolf pack, you go for the leaders, right? Both vampires and werewolves really need my strategic advice.

From a simple wrist twist, Tiny-Red throws Marco among them like a fabric doll, still passed out. Good. Some of the women, only the pretty ones, are protected behind the wall of furious Alphas. Alisha has some blood splattered on her, and knowing her, I would not be surprised that she jumped in first thing in the fight.

That's the difference between her and me, I suppose. I would have gladly hidden in the bathroom while she was probably trying to overtake the entire vampire army by herself.

Kyle glances at me. I see him acknowledging my broken top, and I know he must have spotted my bruises on the neck. I didn't have time to check them out, but as I swallow again with difficulty, I know how bad they must look. I bet they are already turning purple. I hold his look, hoping for some reaction. As usual, there's only emptiness.

I *know* he knows this is Marco's way. I know he knows I was not agreeable to this. Alisha is too busy comforting other women around her, so she doesn't see me yet. I can't wait for her to hear my way of thinking about her amazing suggestion. My legs are still shaking from the encounter with Marco, and I barely hold back my tears. If this asshole thinks I'm gonna stay silent, he's wrong.

Too bad we are surrounded by those damn vampires. Kyle is still watching me, unimpressed, when his look freezes. I think maybe the screaming vibes I sent through my mind worked and reached his little pea.

"Which one of my boys did that to you?" someone asks.

With a gasp, I jump around. I am done being sneaked up on. Then I see him.

Tall, dark, handsome—an actual fucking cliché of a vampire. His eyes are bright red. His pupil is dark and in the shape of a snowflake—which is kind of yuck. Both sides of his head are shaved and displaying tattoos. What is left of his hair on the top is braided, the braid reaching far below his shoulders, from where I can see.

I stay silent, still observing, taking in the unreal beauty. I can die happy. I met a vampire, and he's hot. I wish I could ask him about garlic and coffins, but it doesn't seem like the right moment. After Marco's attack, a bit of watching can't hurt.

His skin is a bit creepy, so white it is almost translucent, and his veins are close to dark, going from light purple to dark aubergine, as if some kind of sickness moves through his body.

"I asked a question, Little Wolf." The Sexy-Cliché raises an eyebrow.

"I found her like this," Tiny-Red says, "with Sleeping Beauty there." He nods toward Marco, who has awakened between the last time I saw him and now, and looks at the vampire and me like we were both mortal diseases.

"Hmm." In a movement so fast I can't see it coming, the vampire's hand is surrounding my neck, but instead of the atrocious pressure I expect to feel again, a caress as soft as a feather tickles me. His thumb strokes my damaged throat up and down. Then, as fast as before, his hand is gone, leaving an icy feeling over my skin. Breathless.

He bends his head over me, whispering to my ear so low even I can barely make out the words. "Your blood is driving me insane... Go stand with your people, Little Wolf, before I decide to taste you down below."

I squeal and step back to the small space left among the wolves behind me. I try not to pay attention to the whispers, and I sure hope nobody heard him. At least I have Alisha's attention now, her eyes quickly running over my body, then to Marco. She pouts, holding my glare, and sighs.

Seriously, girl? You're giving me the pout? *Me*?

Sexy-Cliché still has his eyes on me, staring, his head leaning to the side, as if he is deep in reflection. He turns his attention, and without a tremor in his voice, he addresses the room. "Wolves. It's a pleasure." And there it is, a big, bright smile with two fangs growing to a decent length right under our eyes.

I can't decide if this is on the creepy side or the fascinating side. And also, I quickly wonder if fang size matters for vampires? This existential question goes straight to my list of 'questions to be answered before I die.'

I sure hope no more of them are going to make a comment about my period; the thought makes me uneasy. I cross my arms over my chest, realizing the state of my outfit. Deep inside, I hope Alisha won't be the only one to guess what has happened with Marco. Maybe, just maybe, others will take my defense when I speak up.

"I'm Viggo, King of Vampires." His smile is even bigger now, and he accompanies his words with a large gesture of his arms.

As an answer, his army sings 'woop woop woop!', which I don't think is particularly vampire-like. Tiny-Red is particularly excited. I'm guessing he's fan number one of Viggo.

"So... this"—he nods around the room—"was my introduction." He pauses, fixing his crimson eyes on our alphas. "You are getting... regrouped... how funny. I'm sure you will understand why some of my peers can't see the use for it."

The question was directed at Kyle, who stands silent for one second before deciding to wear his balls and answer.

"You have been regrouping for millennia." Kyle retorts, "and now, you have a king. It's our right to protect ourselves. That's why we are getting together."

That is true. I remember the accounts of slaughter told by some of our new members.

The king seems to consider the question seriously, taking what seems like minutes to answer, as if he were deciding whether or not to burn us all. "If any *unjustified* attack against wolves were to happen, I would deal with it myself. Give me a name, give me a location, and I am ready to personally hunt down those vampires."

He crosses his hands behind his back and walks around the room, so elegant that he looks like a ballet dancer on ice skates. A ballet dancer with tattoos, Viking hair, and a nice ass.

Some older members in the pack whisper to each other. I know this is unprecedented, but I'm hoping that everyone can be... friends? The mortal enemies concept is so 20th century. While he's talking, I stare at Sexy-Cliché, who continues his little speech.

"Also, we have been observing you for a little while, and there are two things that need to change."

I can see that Kyle is ready to argue with whatever comes, and I thank Alisha for placing her hand on his arm, warning him with her eyes to shut the fuck up.

You go, girl! Oh, wait, I forgot I hate her.

The king looks in their direction too, and he chuckles, not disturbed. "First thing, there have been accidents on a full moon. Hikers, party students, and wolves are getting out of the woods. How hard can it be to stick to a tree and do your needs there?"

I want to scream at him that he's an asshole, but I don't think that would help. We are not dogs! There have been accidents, though, and I hate that he's right; innocents have been killed.

Oh, wait.

"But you're killing many people, more than us." Oh no. Did I say that aloud? Everyone in the room is staring at me.

Viggo speeds toward me, making me jump *again*. "Little Wolf... what makes you say that?" he asks, a smirk on his lips, his eyes following the curves of my body until they fix for one second on my crotch.

Geez.

I blink two or three times, and I gesture around the room, holding back a 'duh.'

He looks around as well, stopping his eyes on some bodies. "Oh. I see. True. We love to kill. We made a statement here, but we, unlike your pack, make sure to hide our bodies after we kill them."

"Sooo... maybe when my pack kills someone, by *mistake*, they can also hide the body, can't they?" I need to slow down. I know I need to, but I can't stop. Today's not the day.

Tiny-Red hides his laughter behind the king's back; I can see him, and I want to throw him my shoe. I see Kyle from the corner of my eye moving toward us, stopped instantly by two other vampires growling at him.

"Excuse her," he says from afar. "She's a bit... special."

I scoff and I'm ready to throw my other shoe at him, but what the king says next interrupts me.

"I know."

Now he's the one I'm looking at, unsure how to react.

"I'm. Not. Crazy!" I shout while poking his chest with my index finger.

Viggo wears an abashed look on his face, as if he is surprised to be touched, and laughs. At me, I'm guessing. He continues speaking, addressing the crowd but keeping his eyes on me. "Wolves watching out for their kills on the full moon is the first thing you are going to amend. The second thing is, I heard... an interesting rumor." This time, his looks deviate toward my broken strap.

I tentatively try to put it back in place, which is, of course, impossible, given that Marco has destroyed it. I release my shoulder strap and instead aim to tidy my rebel curl behind my ear.

"You wolves would not be stupid enough to create Omegas now, would you?" the king asks.

When I raise my eyes to look at him, his eyes are shining, his pupils entirely dilated, almost covering the crimson with the darkness. I raise my head, holding his look. What am I supposed to say? Thankfully, dear Kyle always has something to say.

"We don't have Omegas in this pack." Kyle almost sounds as if he believes his lie.

I scoff involuntarily, and to hide it, I fake a cough in my elbow. I know this can't have escaped the king.

Viggo doesn't smile. Instead, he turns toward Kyle. "Is that so? I'm guessing rumors were wrong then." He gives Kyle a full, toothy smile, fangs out. "If a pack were to demote someone to Omega, I would have to take preventive measures."

The silence is awkward. I know if I say something, not only will I be a snitch, but I have enough problems as it is. I would get everyone slaughtered, and we have families in this house. This is wolf's business.

I wish someone would at least ask the question, 'why?' are Omegas a forbidden thing? Like, come on? Pretty please? A girl needs to have all the ammunition before going into battle. I can already see myself out of this shit, imagining how I am going to threaten Kyle and the others to set me free. *Bye, fuckers!*

"Why would vampires care about our class system?" Marco asks in a hideous voice, standing proudly, as if he hadn't been carried like a puppy five minutes earlier by a tiny vampire. I'm going to cherish the image in my mind for the rest of my life.

"We don't," Viggo answers, "what we care about, though, is what usually follows."

Silence falls in the room.

Gosh, I hate people who don't finish their freaking train of thought. I glance at Marco; he is silent and staring at the vampire. I can tell he's grumpy. Note for myself: do not get in his way for at least three days.

"And?" I ask, biting my lips when Viggo turns his look swiftly toward me. "What... follows?"

"Insanity, my dear Little Wolf. Insanity."

That is still not helpful. I give up. Men, either they talk too much, or they don't talk enough.

Viggo finally goes away from me, turning his back, and I try not to let my eyes follow the hard curves of his body. His shoulders are large, and I can guess the muscle through his elegant shirt. His hair is the longest I have ever seen in a man, reaching the end of his back, right above his bottom. A bottom, which I can't appreciate long enough as he rotates on his heels, dancing, and clapping his hands.

"So, wolves, this is what's going to happen," he says. "For the next few full moons, we will watch you, and we will place a protective spell around your territory just to make sure you behave. Don't worry, we will stay outside the barrier."

The pack starts to become agitated. Having vampires around us at a full moon is not the idea of the century. Not that I care. I am pretty sure I would not smell a damn vampire in the forest even if I tried.

Viggo continues. "If I hear little birds talking about this new caste system of yours... I'll kill you all."

CHAPTER 6

LYING ON MY THIN mattress on the floor, I stare up at the stained ceiling.

Miraculously, we survived the vampires' visit. Well, let's say most of us did.

We buried our dead at the end of our garden, right before the forest starts, though I wasn't invited to the ceremony. No surprise there. Not like there's anyone left I would shed a tear for anyway.

I have more important things to do. I have to think about what the threat from Viggo means for me. This is my time to shine.

The Alphas surely won't do anything stupid... will they? I want to believe that, but deep down, I know better. At the thought of Marco's hands on my body, tears fill my eyes. Now that the first shock of the vamp attack is gone, shame flows through me. A sob escapes my mouth. I want to be hopeful,

I really do, but the vampires won't have any idea what's happening here if the Alphas are smart enough to hide it.

Unfortunately, seeing how little I trust my Alphas right now, an escape seems like the best plan.

I don't have time to reflect more on this when I hear the unmistakable crack on the stairs leading to my room. This might be a cliché, but yes, I have obviously been moved into the attic. My breath catches in my throat. No one ever comes to visit me. Not since I was demoted to Omega.

I jump to my feet, my pulse racing. No way am I presenting myself in a weak position. I grab a knife I stole from the kitchen, my fist clenching on the wooden handle. If they're trying to take me down, I'll slice a few of their cocks first.

My thoughts fly through the roof; the instinct of running away is too strong. The window is high, but the jump is still doable.

The door opens slowly, and I brace myself.

It's not a vampire. It's worse.

In walks Kyle, flanked by the other Alphas. Their faces are stern, but their eyes are calculating. They are so big that my room feels tighter by the second. My grip on the knife tightens, and my heart keeps hammering. Now that they're here, I'm not sure I want to find out why.

Kyle's eyes flick to the knife in my hand. He smirks. "Still fighting, Mina? You don't really need it with us, but good. You'll need that fighting spirit."

I scoff and nod my knife toward Marco. "He knows why I need it," I spit. "I can't believe you are letting him get away with it."

Kyle doesn't care about my last comment. He *doesn't care.* "We need to talk," he says, his voice steady, authoritative.

I can't help the frown on my face, but he interrupts me before I can say a word.

"About your role in this... situation with the vampires."

I scoff, stepping back. "My role? I thought I didn't have one anymore, you know, forbidden caste system and all." I know I sound like a victorious bitch, and I also know I'd better watch my next steps carefully.

One of the other Alphas—James, a hulking brute of a man—chuckles darkly. "Oh, you've got a role now, Omega. You'll be helping us get close to the king."

My blood runs cold. "What?"

Kyle steps forward, the amusement at my little rebellion gone from his face. "We need you to seduce the king. Get close to him; find out his weaknesses. And when he trusts you, we need you to get something from him. A watch."

I blink, my heart thudding in my chest. "A... watch?" It sounds ridiculous, like some weird role-play game, but the way Kyle's jaw clenches tells me it's anything but.

"Don't ask questions about the watch," James growls. "Just get it."

I swallow hard, trying to process what they're asking. "Okay... first thing. He's a millennial vampire. He probably has no weaknesses. Second, I highly doubt he will trust some random wolf from the enemy pack he just threatened to death. And third, even if, by some miracle, he trusts me, I guarantee you there's no way in hell he would let me access this... watch if this is something so important."

"Stop being a little whiny bitch," Marco says.

I give him my baddest, bitchiest look. It doesn't work. "I'm not being a whiny bitch; I'm being a smart one," I retort.

"For some reason, he seemed to find you fuckable," Marco says.

I want to punch him for those words. A bit hypocritical, considering he thought I was good enough to be forced on earlier.

Marco continues. "Just go to him, seduce him, open those pretty little legs of yours, and give him this sweet pussy you're holding onto. That should do it."

"Yeah, no. I don't think I want to do that—"

Kyle cuts me off, his tone icy. "If you do this, Mina, we'll reinstate your status in the pack. No more Omega. No more debts. You'll be free. Stay or leave; we don't care. Just get him to trust you. He was showing interest in you for some reason; this might be easier than you think. Vampires love virgin blood. You might not even have to sleep with him."

He sure knows how to talk to a woman.

The word *'free'* hits me like a punch to the gut. I feel a sharp sting of hope, immediately followed by dread. Seduce a vampire? Get close enough to steal from him? The thought makes my skin crawl. The king didn't survive for so long by being fooled by a pretty pair of legs and some long eyelashes.

But... freedom. No more being a servant, no more scraping by on leftovers. No more dirty laundry, no more being looked down on by everyone who used to be my family. I could have my life back without having to hide from them the rest of my life. *That* sounds pretty good.

My mind turns at a rapid speed. I will probably have to hide from vampires. They can only go out at night, so... I'm guessing that's a win? If I head to a sunny part of the country, it will give me more chances to survive.

I look at Kyle, searching his face for any sign that this could be a trick. No, he seems serious.

"The king said there was no caste system allowed. You heard him. So, I don't think I should care about your threat now, should I?" I ask, my voice quieter, knowing very well this is it. Whatever their answer is, it will make the decision for me.

The air in the room grows heavier.

Marco steps forward, his towering frame casting a shadow over me, his eyes turning an ochre color other werewolves have when shifting. "You *don't* want to refuse."

Kyle sighs, a look of false sympathy crossing his face. "Look, Mina, this is the only way you can prove your worth. Maybe we won't call you Omega, but we will still treat you the same. Or worse."

"Worse?" I ask, unsure there's worse.

From the dark look they all send me, I know exactly what they're really talking about. If I'm alive, I won't let a single one of those fuckers touch me ever again. I'm ready to retort when I'm interrupted.

"We need the watch, Mina; that's all we're asking," another Alpha—Leon, one of the quieter ones—speaks up, his voice laced with something I can't quite place. He holds up a book, its pages yellowed and frayed, smelling faintly of dust and death. "There's a prophecy. The watch is necessary for our pack to survive this. The vampire threat... it's all written here. I'm still working through the translation, but it says the watch belongs to us. Vampires stole it ages ago. We just need it back to ensure our survival. We need the odds to become a bit more equal."

"Really?" I scoff, trying to mask my fear with sarcasm. That's the first time I've heard of this. "Now we're following old books? You have been basing the last few weeks on this thing. Look where it got us; this damn book is literally the reason why we were attacked."

I am curious, but if I show that I'm curious, I'll never get my hands on the book.

Kyle steps closer, his eyes hard. "Do you want our species to survive?"

Honestly, I'm not sure.

He continues. "You may be useless as a wolf and as a girlfriend, but maybe you can still bring your... contribution to the pack."

I glance at the book in Leon's hands, marked with strange symbols and Post-it notes showing between many of the pages. I can't read the language, but the pages hum with something ancient, something that makes my stomach twist in knots. I don't like this book. If it were me, I would throw it into the fire. Do they hear this strange sound coming from it? Have those guys ever watched Evil Dead??

"So... what?" I ask. "I'm supposed to throw myself at a vampire and hope he doesn't kill me first? All of this for a watch, and you won't tell me what it's for?"

Kyle's expression softens, but it's not kindness—it's manipulation. I know his face by heart. "No, you're going to be smart about it. Get close to him. Use that pretty face of yours and then... When the time's right, take the watch. There's nothing more. We just need to keep the watch here, with us. For safety."

I hesitate, biting the inside of my cheek. The thought of being caught by a vampire while stealing from him terrifies me. But what terrifies me more is staying here, stuck as an Omega, forever at their mercy. Even though vampires said we could not have a caste system, Kyle has confirmed that I didn't need the title to get the same treatment.

If you're asking me, they're all enjoying my situation a tad too much.

And if I fail, well, then I run far and fast. With both of the most dangerous creatures on Earth in my pursuit. Can't wait!

My silence stretches on, and Kyle presses again, his voice dropping lower. "Do this, and you'll be one of us again, free if you wish to be. Do nothing... and you'll stay at the bottom. One way or another. Forever. If you think anyone in this house is going to help you, think again. Unlike you, they know a threat when they see one. The vampires just started this war."

I look down at the knife clutched in my hand. I could stab Kyle right here and now, but what good would it do? He will heal in a few hours anyway, asshole.

I remember Viggo's eyes, his incredible presence. He's the one who doesn't like this caste system. Maybe I should indeed become a friend.

I look up at Kyle and nod, letting out a shaky breath. "Fine. I'll do it."

Kyle's lips curl into a smile—satisfied, smug. "Good girl."
Asshole.

As they leave, the door clicks shut behind them. I drop back onto my bed, my mind racing. My decision is made.

I smirk. A prophecy? A vampire? And me... definitely not a good girl.

CHAPTER 7

OUR PACK HAS JUST reached the forest in our human forms, but the others are already feeling the call of the moon pulling at their entrails. Except me. I try to add a wince of pain to my face, but my acting skills are nowhere near good enough, not when I have so many thoughts on my mind.

I stand at the edge of the woods, my heart pounding in my chest. My eyes follow the various shadows falling onto the ground. The others tremble, their extremities changing as their wolves take over.

The Alphas made their offer, and I made my decision.

There is no hesitation in my mind. Tonight is the night. I swallow hard. I forced myself the last few days to act normal, asking enthusiastic questions about how to get to the king, while making sure none of the Alphas ever trapped me alone. For them, this is just another night beneath the moon, but for me, this is the night when I take back my freedom.

While also adding a pinch of pain in their neck.

I hide in the shadows, stepping back into the trees, letting my eyes roam around. I'm searching for our fangy babysitters. Vampires. We know they're here. I couldn't smell them on our way to the forest, but our Alphas did. They didn't like this one bit; I could see anger twisting on their faces. Tonight is absolutely a night when I have to hide.

For my plan to go right, I need those vampires out of my way. Hopefully, they won't pay attention to my wolf. Something I haven't thought about is the magical barrier they used. This could become a problem, but it's okay. I'll wait until the first rays of the sun, when the barrier lowers, and when the members of my pack are screeching in pain. Then? I'd better run fast. They won't be looking for me. They never do.

My steps are steady as I walk deeper into the forest, glancing over my shoulder, making sure none of them witness my shifting. When I hear the faraway growls lowering, I take off my simple dress and shift without hesitation, feeling a sense of warmth, a sense of being home. I dig my paws into the dirt, enjoying the life beneath the ground. I stretch my back paws until I push, heading toward the falls for a last goodbye, a final hiding for the night.

The air is alive with the rustle of leaves and the distant calls of nocturnal creatures. My senses are sharp, every sound and scent amplified by the tension thrumming through my veins. I can hear the damn bunnies I can't catch running by my side. *Seriously, guys?*

I arrive at the falls and feel it before I see it—the presence of someone larger, something dangerous. I stop. The bunnies run away, back into the trees. As a low growl rumbles through the trees, I see him: a massive wolf, its fur dark as midnight, its eyes burning with danger. *Marco.*

I have seen him in his wolf shape before and promised myself to always avoid him. Well, until tonight.

The creature's movements are careful and predatory, circling me. My instincts scream at me. With Marco, this can't be good. I thought it was clear I was out of this now, with the secret mission and all. I hold my ground, my breath shallow, but terror takes over. My wolf can't do anything against him.

The wolf lunges, its teeth snapping inches from my face, and I spin away, my body reacting before my mind can catch up. I run. Or at least I try. A heavy weight falls onto me. I wince under the burden, my legs crumbling under the bulky beast.

A scream erupts from my throat when his jaws close around my throat. This is a submission bite. *No. No!* I know exactly what this means—this is a male ready to enjoy himself with a female, consent or not, who cares. I try to wrench myself away, my paws scrabbling uselessly on the ground. He's too strong. For a fleeting second, I consider shifting back and screaming with all my lungs—maybe the shock would give me an edge? Not to mention, our babysitters would probably intervene. At this point, I'm choosing vampires over werewolves.

My vision blurs as tears spill from my eyes. Something hard pokes me from behind. In a last survival instinct, I kick back, playing rodeo with the wolf above me, reaching his nose with my teeth in a contorted move.

A pained growl erupts behind me.

I don't wait.

The forest blurs around me as I sprint. Behind me, the wolf is already chasing; of course, my bite was not that painful for him. It just pissed him off. I can hear his snarls and growls filling the darkness behind me. Fear claws at my chest, but survival is my drug right now. I can't let him catch me. I won't. I need to reach the vampires.

The thought comes from nowhere: *If only I could fly.*

And something... *shifts.*

A surge of power I have never felt before. My body contorts, my limbs changing shape as I shriek with a mix of fear and excitement. As usual, there is no pain but only this blessed feeling, and exhilaration mingles as feathers erupt from my skin.

What in the living hell?

I leap into the air, and without a doubt, I know what to do. Wings spread wide. I can feel the wind beneath me carrying me higher and higher, leaving an angry Marco below, howling at the night, calling other members of our pack.

Not today, asshole.

My heart hammers in my chest, half from terror, half from awe. I glance down and catch the glint of white wings in the moonlight. I'm pretty sure I'm an owl. A damn owl. Definitely not a werewolf.

There must be no magical barrier in the sky because I don't feel a thing as I continue my elegant flight, catching a glimpse below from some shadows. Vampires watch with interest toward the edge of the forest.

The forest stretches out beneath me until I spot our mansion in the distance, my resolution certain. I aim for an open window and shift mid-flight, my body contorting, my wings folding into arms, legs, and skin. I stumble inside—into Kyle's room. My breath comes in ragged gasps, and I'm shaking all over, but I've never felt more *alive*.

I scan the room—my old room—and there it is.

The book.

The one no one ever let me touch. The one that smells so wrong. The one that needs to go.

I snatch it up, my hands trembling. No time to pack. No time to think. Besides the expensive pen I stole from Kyle, I don't have any possessions worth risking my life for.

I run toward the windows and take a deep breath. *Come on, I need to do it again.*

Relief floods through me as I transform again. The white wings return, and my face rounds. With no further ado, I catch the book between my brand-new claws and fly away in the night, my powerful wings carrying me. The house shrinks behind me. In the distance, I hear angry howls; the wolves still stuck in their magical cage.

I don't look back. There's nothing left for me there.

Whatever this damn book is about, I'm gonna make sure no werewolves ever find it again.

CHAPTER 8

6 months later

I TILT THE BOTTLE, filling the glass with a steady hand, focusing on the amber liquid, enjoying the rough smell reaching my nose. Lifting my head, I quickly scan the room, assessing the patrons present tonight. It's Saturday night in New Orleans, a few days before Halloween, and the fancy bourbon bar I work in is as busy as it gets. Jazz music pours from the speakers. A group of obvious tourists in matching 'I love New Orleans' T-shirts laugh loudly after their third glass of bourbon.

I smile to myself. I love this. I enjoy the anonymity. I like the crowd dancing and singing around me as I walk through the streets day and night. Most of all, I enjoy guessing vampires in the streets. Weird creepy skin? Yep. Disco shirt? Probably. Hungry looks? Hell yeah.

It has been six months since I ran away from the pack. I'm becoming a bit more like myself day by day, enjoying my newfound freedom, growing more confident as the days pass. I have stopped glancing over my shoulder, waiting for the shadows to hurt me. Nightmares are also becoming more sparse over the nights. I used to wake up screaming, covered in sweat, feeling the reach of their claws around my ankles, of their sweaty hands pinning me down. Those nightmares have almost gone now.

The only downside to this new life? I am free, but I am not wealthy. Rent is too expensive in the city. But, hey, at least I'm happy. And still a horny virgin.

Those fuckers thought they would throw me to the king? Haha! Joke's on them. In New Orleans, the city is ruled by witches and vampires, sharing the benefits of the legends surrounding this place about the occult. It's invaded by millions of tourists every year. And more importantly? I knew from a new guy in the pack that werewolves are not allowed here. So, where did I go? Right in the middle of the French Quarter. Vampire Town.

After all, I don't need to shift on the full moon anymore, so it's easy to hide. I have been training on my shifting gift as well, or whatever this is. The flight away from home was incredible. I was close to enjoying being a bird even more than being a wolf until I remembered how it felt to feel the mud between my paws. I tried to be a cat for a little while. I love cats. Being a stray cat in a city like this is no fun and unsafe; other cats were always looking for trouble, so I had to stop.

I am far from the pack and even farther from the king. When I arrived here, I heard that he lives in Alaska, in Juneau or somewhere similar.

I haven't spotted a single werewolf since I landed, and I'm fine with it. I have done everything to disappear, to melt into the crowd. I dyed my hair brown and cut my hair to shoulder length to blend in. I cried when I did it, obviously, and I miss my red curls, but safety first.

No one's looking for a redheaded wolf here.

"Oh, hey, have you seen a redheaded wolf?"

"No, bro, ain't no redhead wolf in New Orleans."

I managed to miraculously find a job as a waitress in one of the multiple bourbon bars of the city, right in the busiest touristy neighborhood. John, the manager, gave me a chance despite the poor image I must have shown the first time we met. He's trying to be lenient with my incapacity at not breaking glasses, and I know it's because he feels bad for me.

He's a vampire. He told me that the first day he hired me, even though I already knew he was one—pale skin, a disco shirt, and a hungry look. John always tells his employees what he is, and then he hypnotizes them to force them to never tell the secret. According to their reaction to the big announce-ment, he also sometimes hypnotizes them to forget all about it and sends them away. My reaction must have shocked him because when he told me, I was really not that impressed.

'It's okay, that's cool,' apparently doesn't fill the list of proper reactions to a big vampirism secret.

It didn't matter that he was a bloodsucker because after a few weeks in the city, I understood that vampires had rules to follow. Like, a *lot* of rules. They don't seem inclined to break them, but then, if a scary king were the one to make laws, I would follow them, too.

Therefore, I love it here. Maybe seventy percent of the locals in the French Quarter are vampires or witches. They work together to keep the tourism running high so that the blood never runs low. It's a free buffet for everyone, but guess what? It works.

Something even better? If you're a mortal but living here locally, you have the possibility to visit a witch to ask for what they call a 'Local Bracelet.' This is a silver bracelet with a stone—mine is a lapis lazuli—and it says to any random vampires that you're under the protection of the city—and of the scary king. No need to say that as soon as I learned about this, I went straight for it. John is the one who told me about it, which screams 'green flag' as far as bosses go. I obviously didn't mention the whole 'shifter' thing.

I'm happy.

"Shit!" I scramble while taking the glass to the customer, my feet stuck against the bag strap of another one, and it's with an exploding heartbeat that I watch the scene in slow motion. My expensive glass of bourbon falls and splashes on a customer.

To make matters even better, it splashes onto the shirt of the scariest man I have ever seen in my life. *Fuck. The King.*

It has been six months, but he didn't change, which is a silly comment to make, as he is a vampire. Duh. Still tall, still handsome in a creepy way, still scary as fuck. I let out a whine when his eyes settle onto me, and he shows no sparkle of recognition.

Please let this be a miracle.

His chest is now covered with the expensive bourbon, already soaking through. I fear the storm coming, but he stays surprisingly quiet. Is there such a thing as penetrating eyes? I sure feel penetrated. I lower my gaze while trying to wipe his even more expensive shirt with my dirty rag, hoping he won't recognize me. Maybe the hair trick will be enough.

In the middle of my stupid mumbles of excuses, his sultry voice stops me, bringing a tremor from the depths of my soul.

Dramatic much?

"It's all good, darling; I'll take care of it."

Right. If he is smart, he knows his shirt is not getting any cleaner with this dirty rag.

"I am so, so, so sorry," I stammer, still keeping my eyes low until I make the mistake of looking up, wanting to judge how much trouble I am in.

We're fixed on each other for what feels like an eternity until I take a deep breath, panicking. He does not seem bothered in the least by it. His lips draw the sexiest smile I have ever seen.

Oh, gosh, my poor heart. How can one have purple veins and be so sexy?

Someone chuckles to his right. Tiny-Red. *Double-fuck.*

The redhead is holding his glass in the most nonchalant way, not showing any recognition. I'm guessing that when you have met thousands of women in your life; maybe you just forget about them.

Let's not take a chance on that. I stand up, biting my lips, and mumble about bringing another glass. I don't take a step when Sexy-Cliché grabs my hand.

"Why don't you bring your number while you're at it, pet?" His lips move, but I don't hear them. I *feel* him. I feel his touch on me like I would feel a wave swallowing me whole and throwing me back onto dry, painful sand. I can't breathe, and I pull my hand away as naturally as possible and mumble again about the fresh drink coming his way while turning on my heels.

I walk fast toward the counter, where I see John's disapproving look, with this slight movement of the head he always does when I fail at something. The poor man—vampire—has been so patient with my mishaps.

"I'm sorry, John. I tripped on a bag."

"This can't continue, sweetie. You know I have to take this off for your pay, right? This damn Bourbon is a hundred bucks a glass."

My eyes widen. I can't afford that. "Can I clean dishes instead? I need the money, John."

Is it okay to beg in front of dozens of customers? I sure think it is. John is already shaking his head, and I can feel the tears coming up. I know he feels bad, but he runs a business. I also know that some of the other staff are jealous of his lenient side toward me, as obviously I am paid the same for much less talent. One hundred dollars off it is, then. I guess I'm nowhere close to being able to afford a flat.

A voice I recognize interrupts us: "I'll pay for the broken glass and wasted Bourbon, John." Viggo is behind me. I can feel his presence smothering me. I turn toward him, eyes wide open, and damn, he's even hotter than the first time. Especially when he offers to pay.

John seems to have a slight second of panic, probably recognizing his king. He nods, bowing so slightly that it's barely noticeable.

I try to wipe my single tear that escaped. "Thank you; you didn't have to."

Viggo stares at my face, and for once, I wish he were looking at my boobs, as the other clients do. He smiles and raises his hand to my face. I straighten, ready for another wave of weirdness to come through, but he brushes my cheek so lightly I don't feel a thing.

"I think I'm owed a phone number now." His smile becomes playful, and that's terrifying.

"Right."

This is a terrible idea, I know, but I still scribble my number on a coaster.

You just gave your number to the freaking king you're trying to avoid! I scream in my head, but it's too late.

Sexy-ass-vampire has already stolen the coaster, and with a turn, he leaves. He goes back to his friend, who is waiting patiently at their table. He didn't recognize me; I'm sure of it. He would have said something, right?

Bye-bye, peace of mind.

CHAPTER 9

AFTER A FEW MORE hours of torture and at the end of the worst shift of my life—drama queen? Me? Absolutely not—I manage to leave with no cut on my paycheck, and more importantly, $300 in tips. Let's not mention that Mr. King of Vampires is the one who gave me a beautiful fifty-dollar bill. This one is going straight into my special savings, the one I keep for finally being able to afford a freaking deposit for a rental flat. I love a man who tips properly.

I could already be in a beautiful, fancy flat, where no deposit was needed, but I ran away because of the flatmates: vampires.

I remember, as if it were yesterday, entering a nest and feeling like I would be the next meal. Three of them were indeed looking for a flatmate/snack, and they said I smelled delicious, in a snack-for-vampire way, I guess. No need to say that I politely refused the offer, and I ran away. Thankfully, the sun was still out, so they didn't follow me.

A few days later, I found my job and learned about the amazing idea of a Local Bracelet. I'm sure any other girl would not mind having free rent and being fed on, but I sure do. I know it's their food, but it seems way too intimate for me to roll with it. An accident can quickly happen, and then, bye-bye Mina. Survived an army of psycho Alphas, succumbed as a snack.

Unfortunately, it means that between them and the squat of an empty, dirty, decrepit building, well, I had to go with the building. Nobody else would take a tenant without a deposit or some kind of physical favours.

Yep, I am homeless—kind of. I can't really complain, seeing that I have a roof above my head, and my existing flatmates are all, believe it or not, adorable. I luckily stumbled on them right when I was running away from the snack-for-vampire situation, and they offered me a place to stay.

I see my friends from the start of our cul-de-sac, and immediately my spirits lift. I'm not thinking about my awful lack of waitressing skills, nor am I thinking about Mr. King. While I get closer, I spot Anya, Ms. Marble, and Cherie all around the metal barrel they use as a table. I am done with my shift, but I can guess from their clothes that they are ready to start theirs.

"Hi, girlfriend!" exclaims Ms. Marble in her deep voice. Tonight, she wears an absolutely indecent electric blue dress that does not leave anything for the brain to imagine. She is busy knitting some rainbow-looking scarf, one of her passions, even though New Orleans weather doesn't exactly call for knitted scarves.

"Hi," I answer back, getting a quick hug from all of them. The mix of perfumes and smoke gets to my head.

Cherie takes one step back from the hug and examines me from head to toe, her purple wig following her movements. Her stare is so intense that I feel myself blushing.

"Uh, Ooooh, someone has some tales to tell, ladies!"

Giggles and wooo screams answer to her, and I scoff, shaking my head, knowing very well that I am not going to get out of this so easily.

I sigh. "Nothing big, I swear! Just... this guy..."

More giggles reach my ears, and I can see their excitement. My friends sadly all gave up on the idea of finding love. I still haven't, but they are quite hopeful they could live it through me, even though the few dates I had since I arrived were all bad and reeking of despair. They're still hoping.

I bring my hands to the barrel, flicking my fingers on it, and tell the story, describing my sexy-ass-vampire in detail. He won them over with the 'no cut on the paycheck for Mina.' I finished them off with my brand new fifty-dollar bill that I proudly show.

"This is going straight to our 'flat fund'" I proudly say, waving my beautiful bill in their faces.

Anya claps with excitement.

"I think by Christmas we should be able to afford one! Even just two bedrooms! And by March next year I'll finally graduate, then I'll find a job that doesn't request any cocks in my pussy, and with my first pay, I'm treating you ladies to a fancy dinner!"

Anya has been studying part-time for a bookkeeping degree—someone told her there were lots of jobs for it, and she's good with numbers. We are all hoping to be out of the street in six months time.

Amid the laughs, Cherie turns to me and says, "Darling, I am going to give you advice that I wish someone had told me when I was young and beautiful like you."

"Oh God, here she goooes," Anya says, throwing her dark hair above her shoulders.

Cherie shushes her with a gesture of her manicured hands. Her long nails are showing off pretty little pearls today. "Let me resume. The guy is sexy as hell but also kind of cute. He has money, he has *manners*, and he is potentially interested in you?"

"Well... he just asked me for my number. It really means nothing. And oh my god, Cherie, you know I don't really care about money." I pause for a minute before biting my lips. "I do care that he didn't yell at me, though."

Even though he's the king of vampires with a reputation to make you blemish. Slaughtering people? It's fine. Yelling at the wait staff? Not on my watch!

"I bet you did!" Ms. Marble chuckles.

They all remember my various accounts of awful nights of my breaking stuff, spilling drinks, and being yelled at by rude customers. Hospitality, ugh. For sure, not screaming immediately at a minimum wage waitress is a good sign, right?

Cherie continues: "If he wants you, go for it. I know you are a bit fussy—"

"I am *not* fussy," I say, outraged, amid the hyena-like laughs of my friends. Not my fault if I have been traumatized by my ex-narcissistic boyfriend and a close-call abuse.

"...it's okay to be fussy," says Cherie. I am ready to protest again, but she interrupts me. "Sweetie, someone like you, so beautiful, so innocent—you are not made for this kind of life." And by saying that, she shoved her head toward our two friends, looking at us with sad smiles, nodding their heads. "And this place, you will grow out of it. You need to start a new life, and if that means being nice to a potentially rich boyfriend, I say you go for it."

"Oh, my god, Cherie!" Anya protests. "You are literally telling her to sell her body while saying that this way she won't end up like us."

"I am not! I am telling her to be smart."

They start arguing about the light difference between prostitution, escorting, and being a sugar baby, and my brain is already fuming.

"Guys... *guys!*" I scream, interrupting their passionate debate. I take a deep breath. "Thank you for your advice, Cherie. I *know* you are right, but I am not gonna force myself if I don't feel it. And remember, we will be out of here soon enough. Also..."

"Also what?" Ms. Marble pushes after my hesitating silence. She has put down her knitting kit while the debate was happening.

"He's a vamp," I mutter.

Well, at least this has the merit of shutting them up. They exchange uneasy looks.

"What?" I sigh.

Ms. Marble is the one to talk. "Okay... sweetie. Vampire?" she whispers, and she gets closer to me. "This could go the right way, or this could go a really, really, *really* bad way."

"I'm guessing with me ending dead?"

"Trust me, if death was the worst, I would tell you to go for it."

Anya intervenes. "They have rules now, Marbie; it's not the same as when we were young." She turns toward me. "I heard their new king is all about rules. I know at least fifty vamps who were killed in the city because they thought they could mess around."

"Well, they still feed on mortals, especially pretty ones like her. I heard vamps love virgin blood." Cherie argues.

Ms. Marble nods.

I can see they're ready to get into an argument about what I should do, so I cut in. Now is not the moment to mention that the guy in question is the freaking king. "Anyway, he has my number, but there is a ninety percent chance that he does not even call."

They all nod. All had their share of men in the past. Common point? They never called back.

I never told my friends about my past. They don't know what I am, what I went through, or what I'm running away from—who I'm running away from. They just know they had to hold me tight during those first few nights when I was screaming in my dreams.

I hope the king won't call, and I'm sure hoping he won't wonder why a fake werewolf is roaming freely in this city.

CHAPTER 10

VIGGO

I HAD TO FOLLOW her. I thought I would have to hide in the shadows to tail her, like any decent predator would, but my Little Wolf does not seem to have the same instinct as your average werewolf.

After she dropped her glass on me, on any other occasion, with any other person, really, I would have blasted them with my look and probably kept them for a later snack. Especially when the snack in question is so gorgeous. When those almond-shaped green eyes stared at me, already filled with tears threatening to explode, I could not do much besides being soft. Gregory found this hilarious. I am sure that not only will he make fun of me later, but he will probably tell the story to his wife: my unbearable sister, Maggie. The two of them together should be forbidden.

I sigh, rolling my eyes at the thought of the talk that was about to come, and return my attention to the redhead. Well. The brunette now. Mina. Even her name is perfection.

The bookworm guy in me can't stop thinking about the Mina of Dracula, who, funnily enough, was a good old friend of mine. My Mina is the most beautiful woman I have ever seen, and I have seen many.

There are so many reasons she should be in the jail located in my house right now.

First, she damaged my shirt. And it was a pretty shirt.

Second, it should be a crime to dye your hair when you have the most naturally luscious auburn hair, so bright it reminds me of the sunsets I used to admire as a child.

And third, well... the city is indeed forbidden to werewolves. But here she is. Does she seriously think I would not recognize her? What kind of immortal man would I be if I didn't recognize a woman just because she changed her hairstyle?

I have only been lurking in the shadows for five minutes, but I already know I could spend hours looking at her.

Especially from behind like now, her shiny wavy hair cascading around her shoulders, leaving full space for her perfect apple-shaped butt. I can already imagine grabbing a fist full to better pound her.

At the thought of a naked, begging, squirming Mina under my body, lust rises. The veins on my hands darken as always, my face probably following along. Let's not mention my eyes, likely as red as Mina's old hair.

Should I eat her? Get rid of the temptation once and for all. Her scent promises a fascinating taste, but she is intriguing to me for no obvious reason. That she lives in this decrepit building upsets me, and I am used to not feeling much, but here I am. Feeling. And horny.

Just eat her, I think. I don't need this kind of trouble in my life. That's what Gregory said, too, when he saw me coming back to our table, empty-handed, and with a boner. There is more to it. I am especially intrigued by the whole 'werewolf in hiding in New Orleans' bit.

We made it clear to the witches that they had to keep the detecting spell working at all times of day. Well, they obviously didn't.

I sigh. As king, I have duties, and the biggest one of all is to ensure everyone falls in line when it comes to protecting our identities. Werewolves and witches may not answer to me directly, but I am still planning on controlling them one day. Werewolves running all hairy in the streets? It's just bad for business. Those damn beasts have no control.

I take a few steps back, hiding deeper in the shadows, when the group of women breaks path, my Mina heading toward the building. *Does she really live in this?* The three sex workers head my way, chattering joyfully about their work.

I clench my jaw. Mina should not be here. I have nothing against these women, but my Mina should not have to live in these conditions.

As I walk toward the building, I know she might be enjoying her life here more than the Omega status she had before. I'm almost certain she was the one we heard about. I don't blame her. I can see she's happy here.

She's not the best at her job, she has odd taste in friends, and she is homeless, but I can feel it; she's happier. My little wolf is full of surprises.

Once her friends are out of my way, I move closer to the brick building, glancing at it with a fair amount of skepticism. It looks like the builders gave up halfway through, probably running out of money during the financial crisis.

I pause, listening. I can hear a few heartbeats spread along the five floors, and without a doubt, I know where Mina is headed. It's not that hard to follow once you know the rhythm of one's breathing.

I push on my legs and, without a struggle, I land on one of the scaffolds surrounding the fifth floor. I may be heavy, but I know how to make myself light as a feather. I have been alive—well, dead—for a long time. The metal barely trembles under my weight. I hide in the shadows when I see her. She seems to have her own 'room,' with no door, and which, by the look of it, has been abandoned right in the middle of a painting session. Her scent is all over the place, and I take a deep breath, enjoying the virgin smell looming in the tiny space.

She doesn't spot me at all; for a werewolf, she truly has no instinct. It's quite adorable. That's probably the reason she was picked to be an Omega, besides her beauty.

Omegas are often beautiful women. Alphas know they can have them for pleasure, so they make sure to pick the cute ones, and I have no doubt that's part of the reason she was chosen by her Alpha. *Alphas.*

I know Kyle's pack has been behaving since our visit. We are keeping a close eye on them. In my experience, when Alphas regroup, it's never a good sign for vampires or witches. Wolves are not meant to have more than one leader. It's unnatural, and it breaks their magic. Go and tell that to those hairy balls of anger. They won't listen.

Gregory confirmed to me six months ago that Mina was gone. According to Kyle, they left on 'good terms.' I won't lie, the thought of not knowing where she went disturbed me for a while, but at least she was not an Omega anymore. Her disappearance was for the best. Until now.

I can't hold back a smirk when she lifts her dress past her thighs, then her waist. A growl almost erupts from me when I take a good look at her ass, covered with some pretty black lace panties, holding her splendid curves to perfection.

Damn it. I'm doomed.

CHAPTER II

VIGGO

IMMORTALITY IS A FUNNY thing. Time passes differently when you don't think about death anymore. Hours stretch into days, and days into years, and moments blur into fog. I've stopped pretending I know how many months or years go by. So, if someone asks why I watched her for so long, I will use this as an excuse.

She is curled on her side, her knees brought close to her face. Her breathing is steady, only disturbed by whatever images her brain shows her. I could know all of her dreams and nightmares, but I have been behaving myself and I didn't push through her mind barrier. Her dreams are hers, for now. Even though I would slaughter the entire city just to know what has been making her whine like this for the past five minutes.

Instead, I'm being a reasonable vampire and I stand there, in silence, in the shadows, keeping myself from tasting her.

Thankfully, I don't have time to think more about how her blood would feel on my tongue and how good her pussy would clench around my cock. My phone vibrating against my leg brings me back to reality. I sigh while pulling out the latest technology my sister forced me to buy. I hate phones. I enjoyed the older ones, plugged into a wall; it was convenient, much faster than letters. But these new smartphones? Where anyone can reach you anytime, anywhere? They make my skin crawl.

It's Gregory, and I rarely ignore him.

His message lights up on the screen, and I almost pull a face.

I cast a last look at Mina, who is now back in her peaceful sleep, buried in a mountain of blankets. Judging by the faint musty scent left on those, she must have found them at the closest thrift store. Only her dark hair pokes through the mountain.

It's with regret that I leave the tiny, unfinished bedroom and leap onto the roof of the next building. I land silently, crouched. We can't fly, unfortunately, but old vampires like me usually gain some physical skills after a few centuries. Strength, speed, and grace.

The rooftops of the French Quarter make for easy travel. I leap from one to the next, enjoying the sound of music reaching me from below. It's past ten in the evening, but the night is just starting for our tourists and for vampires.

I quickly reach our house off Bourbon Street, nestled at the end of a quiet cul-de-sac, right in the French Quarter. It's supposed to be our holiday home. We used to live in Alaska most of the year, but I learned that as a king, I will need to be closer to the vampire population.

A few ancient ones are left in Alaska, enjoying being 'lost in the world's asshole,' with just the right amount of people coming through, and darker days for our species. Those were also my reasons for being there. Too bad they started complaining about the sudden influx of vampires coming to their town, wanting to visit me. With some mortal locals asking questions about those weird-looking visitors, I had to adapt.

I love Alaska. It always reminded me of the landscapes of my childhood: the fjords, the open sea, the terrifying mountains, the unpardonable nature. New Orleans is for sure something else. I know Maggie loves it here. She's the one who incited me to move all of our offices here since I have been chosen as king.

When I asked her if she was not missing nature, she answered by shoving a dozen bags from various shops into my arms. She had been busy spending our money.

I smile at the thought when I see her, a statue of perfection. If it weren't for her skin, so lucid one could see through, you would never guess about the pitiless killer inside of her. Maggie is sitting in her favorite chair, the one by the fireplace that inexplicably smells like leather and cinnamon. She's wearing white as per usual, her long, dark hair pulled into a high ponytail. She drinks her favorite cocktail: a Bloody Vamp Mary. You guessed it, it's a Bloody Mary with blood.

I nod at Gregory, who is sitting by her side, barely holding back his eyes from roaming over his wife. They are as besotted with each other as they were when they met.

Not gonna lie, I didn't think much of him when we first met him in the early fifteenth Century. He was the heir of some lord in Scotland, deep in the Highlands, fighting like a demon on a battlefield. We didn't intend to participate; we were just there for fun. When we saw him, a petite redhead full of muscles and fury, we even made a bet about how long he would survive. He was at least one head shorter than all of her clanmates, his kilt displaying his family crest. His chest was bare of any shirt and covered in the blood of his enemies. He had one sword in each hand, but no shield.

"Two swords? He must be compensating for something." I joked to my sister, who was already unimpressed with my sense of humor.

The more time he spent on the battlefield, the more my sister tensed by my side, her eyes red and fixating on him. He valiantly fought against the English. I gave him that, but his clan did not have a single chance to win the battle. In the end, he fell. On his knees, hands clenched on the handle of his heavy swords, his eyes not bowing when the English lord came to him.

I was going to brag to Maggie about winning our bet when she left my side, jumping and landing by his side on the battlefield. She knew very well that we would have to kill everyone in the bloody field, so I stayed there and observed, holding back from rolling my eyes at her.

Her tall, slim figure was covered in a simple white dress—she was already in her white period—her head bowed down onto the defeated, who had his eyes on her, wide open. Neither paid attention to the English army's screaming. A few tried to approach my sister, but they could not even see her movements; she slashed their throats with such speed that it was not visible to the naked eye. Soon, she had slaughtered a few dozen of the English.

In a whisper, she asked, "Do you want this strength? I can offer it to you, my brave one."

It was barely a whisper that escaped his lips, but he had agreed and been by our side for the past five centuries, marrying my sister a few years after the battle. Lucky bastard.

Not so lucky now when I growl at him, showing off the text he just sent me. Greg snickers, unimpressed.

"I had to. That's part of your rules, you know, no werewolves in town."

"I didn't ask you to do it. We don't need anyone to know there's a weakness in our city's magic."

"Don't you want to know what she is doing here?"

"I don't think she's a werewolf. The spell would not have worked."

Maggie interrupts us. "Who the hell are you talking about?"

"The pretty redhead we met at the pack," Greg answers, a smug smile on his lips while he dares to hold my glance.

"The virgin? The Omega?" Maggie asks, suddenly showing more interest in the conversation. "She's here? See, you didn't need to freak out. What about the whole 'werewolves are forbidden' thing?"

After more than a millennium with my twin, I should be used to her annoying comments.

"Yes, sister, this is exactly what we're talking about. Maybe she has a bracelet? The Local one that witches created?" I am talking more to myself than them, but still, I hope for an answer.

Greg smacks his lips. "You're right, I think she does. I saw a stone on her wrist earlier. See. Didn't need to keep watch on those idiots; we found her."

Silence falls for barely a few seconds before Maggie stops it. "Well then, she's not a werewolf. What was she doing with the pack, anyway?"

"Does that mean I threatened the witches for nothing?" Greg thinks aloud, his face showing worry.

"I'm sure they'll forgive you." That was Maggie, showing off a hint of jealousy.

I sat heavily on the couch, my head falling back. I can't believe I have been supporting these two for so long. "Did we hear about her previous pack?" I ask.

Gregory shakes his shoulders. Such a human thing to do. "They're behaving. No caste system seems to be implemented;

they're respecting the boundaries on the full moon. All the Alphas are still there. They would not have let her leave if..."

Maggie gets up, interrupting him. I can feel impatience bubbling in her blood, her veins moving around her entire body in wavy shades of purple, which they always do when she's upset. "That's not good. You know it's not." She's almost blaming me. "You need to stop them. They can't keep a straight mind with so much testosterone in the same pack. We saw it before."

I move back into a better position on the couch. My braid falls onto the side of my face. "I know, but it's important to acknowledge that every species changes over the centuries. Those new multi-alpha packs might not be the same as the one we met 1,000 years ago."

I know she's ready to fight me on this, but I don't want to. I'm trying to be a reasonable vampire king here. If I want the magical world to bow to me one day, I can't have them hate me. I nod to Greg and order him around instead. "Go pick her up in the morning, bring her here. Nicely."

"Why not now?"

Because she needs to sleep. "Because I'm not in the mood right now."

They're both watching me. Maggie's right eyebrow skyrockets to the ceiling in her 'are you lying to me, bitch?' face that she has been practicing for at least four centuries.

"Just do it." I insist, and with no more patience left, I get up and leave the room, not paying attention to the complaints behind me about the sun potion that gives him a headache.

CHAPTER 12

MINA

"ARE WE THERE YET?" I ask for what feels like the hundredth time, leaning back against the sticky leather seat and glaring at Tiny-Red.

That's right, not only did I wake up this morning with his smirking face looming above me—not a nice way to wake up, even though he's cute—but then I was 'invited' to follow him in his car.

By invited, I mean there wasn't much of an option.

Now we're stuck in New Orleans' morning traffic. I thought that if I annoyed him too much, he might let me go.

It hasn't worked yet.

Tiny-Red isn't driving; some other poor guy is. His rapid breathing makes me guess he's mortal and probably wishing he were anywhere but here.

You and I both, bro. You and I.

The car windows are tinted, probably to protect Tiny-Red from the sun, even though I saw him walking in the full sunlight, which I'm quite curious about.

"How come you can walk in the sun?" I ask, since he didn't bother answering my first question. "I thought vampires would melt in sunlight. Or burn. Or explode."

"We do," he replies, turning his head toward me.

I know his name is Gregory. He introduced himself after I threw my pillow at him this morning, which, in my defense, he deserved. His hair is bright red, his face covered with freckles, and his eyes as red as any other vampire. I wonder which color they were before he was turned into a vamp. He may be small for a man, sure, but his broad shoulders and how his arms bulge under his shirt suggest he could probably snap me in half without breaking a sweat.

Tiny but mighty.

"Witches can make a potion for us," Gregory says, "that stops the sun from burning us... For a little while, anyway."

"Wow." Not gonna lie, I'm impressed. I would love to learn more about witches. They seem way more powerful than whatever I was expecting.

"Yep. I don't like it, though; it doesn't seem natural. And if they decide to slaughter us one day by tricking us, we won't see it coming," he adds with a grimace.

I reflect on this for a few seconds before asking, "Then why didn't you wait until night? Or text me? After all, your king has my phone number."

Gregory laughs and slaps his thighs in exaggerated amusement.

"You're funny. You think I had a choice? It seems the king didn't want to wait." He smirks.

He seems to find this funny; I don't. Why does the king want to see me? I hope it has nothing to do with the fact that he knows who I am, but I doubt I am being invited for morning tea. I try to steady my breathing when my thoughts divert onto the king, the way he looked at me six months ago, but also yesterday. Not good. I don't need a psychopathic vamp boyfriend. I glance at Gregory. If they recognized me, they would have said something, right?

I sigh and mutter while returning my attention to the streets, moving faster now that we are out of the traffic.

"What about garlic?" I blurt.

Gregory glares at me. "What about it?"

"Well, can you eat it?"

"Of course, we can eat it. We can eat anything."

"Huh. Interesting."

I go back to looking out the window while he mumbles something about me and my 'stupid questions.'

A few minutes later, the car slows and turns into a cul-de-sac. I see our destination. A New Orleans-style build-ing, gorgeous, and probably out of my price range. Vines ramp above the entire façade, purple flowers blossoming among them, following every walls and balconies.

"This is pretty," I say as the car rolls through the iron gates and onto the square paved court, enclosed on three sides by the brick façades.

"The plants?" Gregory asks, appearing beside my window so suddenly that I nearly scream. He opens the door for me.

I step out, still staring at the house. "Yeah. This is stunning."

He grins, looking oddly proud. "That's my wife's doing."

OMG, is this love I detect? "Is she a vampire? Or a mortal? Do you sleep in the same coffin?"

I may as well throw in my coffin question while I'm at it. I'm way too curious for my own good.

He snickers. "Why? Do you want to join us?"

I let out a strangled squeak and start walking while he con-tinues. "Don't worry, you're going to meet her. She's quite impatient to meet the wolf who makes her brother slow about slaughtering entire packs."

"Brother...?"

A feminine voice interrupts us. "Yes, I have been supporting his ass for a millennium."

I turn to see one of the most beautiful and probably dan-gerous women I have ever met. If her brother is scary to look at, she has an entire vibe that screams, 'I could rip out your intestines while doing my nails and still stay pretty.' She is dressed in a silk white suit, probably costing a few thousand, the jacket hanging open just enough to hint at what's underneath. Or rather, what isn't.

Wow.

The brunette advances toward us. Her hair is the same shade as her brother's. Her skin is also similar to his, her purple veins dancing across her body, and I just realize they seem to be the only vampires with such interesting features. Her sharp heels click against the pavement confidently, while I can barely walk on such unstable ground with my flat boots. Immediately, I feel a change in the mood and witness Gregory's entire attitude changing. They devour each other with their eyes, just holding hands for a second, then turning back their attention to me.

This is what true love looks like.

"So, you're the little wolf, the Omega." Her voice is laced with amusement.

I stop breathing. Should I lie? Deny? Run?

"Maggie!"

Oh well, I can't do any of those things because the king is here, walking toward us. His hair is braided as usual, and he wears leather pants that leave little room for imagination—imagination is already way out of the way—and a black shirt unbuttoned just enough to make me forget about how to talk.

I stay silent, waiting for what's next. There's no point in lying.

"Little Wolf." He smiles, and despite the kindness in his voice, it's terrifying.

"Right. Soooo… you recognized me, I guess." I mumble and look at my feet. Fear claws at my stomach. "I can explain!" I lift my head to meet his crimson stare.

He raises an interrogative brow. "I would *love* to hear your explanation." He has a smug look on his face.

Gregory chuckles. "The witches have confirmed the werewolf spell was still on, but here you are, undetected. It's forbidden."

"Right. Forbidden. Well, technically speaking…" I hesitate.

"Yes, Little Wolf?" He moves closer.

I dive into his red eyes, trying to find some sort of sign about what's coming for me, looking for murder or torture, but his face is close to expressionless. The guy must have been working on his poker face for a while.

"I'm not… *exactly* a werewolf."

The sister snickers, and Viggo hushes her.

"So," I say, "I have the right to be here! Right?" I hold my hands together, anxiously torturing my fingers, trying my best to give my best innocent look.

Viggo stays silent for a little while. "I guess that explains the lack of detection on you."

He raises his hands, and I gasp, the simple gesture reminding me of our first encounter. He moves one of my curls behind my ear, brushing my jawline with his finger. The touch is soft but cold, thanks to his quite dead skin.

"Why would you hide your identity if you knew you had the right to be here?" he asks.

Because I'm running away from a bunch of psychopathic werewolves?

Even though I would love to say that, I'd rather not, so instead I mumble something.

The sister chuckles and says, "Why were you with a pack, then? If you're not a werewolf?"

"I thought I was one... and then... it was too late..."

"...and you didn't want to be alone," the king says, finishing my thought.

I shrug my shoulders. It's true. I didn't want to. I thought I found love and family, but truly, I didn't.

"What about your pack?" Viggo asks, letting his eyes roam over my body.

I tremble under the inspection, under his heavy look, and feel self-conscious of the basic dress I put on in a hurry.

"There's nothing to say; I left them." I tug on the hem of my velvet dress, which is almost the same as my previous favorite, playing with it.

"On good terms?" He stops his analysis of me and raises his head, fixing his crimson pupils on me, his purple veins having their ballet show on his chest, peeking through his open shirt.

"Define 'good terms.'"

"That's what your Alpha, Kyle, said." His poker face went away for a split second right there, and I can detect a coolness in his voice.

I hold back a laugh. "If Kyle said it, then it must be true!"

Viggo does not seem to believe me, which I don't blame him for, seeing that I don't believe myself. I say, "Listen, I don't want any trouble. I am not a werewolf, I don't need to belong to a pack, and obviously, I'm not a danger to anyone in town. I'm perfectly integrated in New Orleans."

"True."

"So... can I go now?"

"Why did you dye your hair?"

"I wanted... some changes. In the modern world, people love to change their look, you know."

"Right. I preferred you as a redhead."

"Well, turns out you don't get a say in it. Listen, I have a shift at three. If we're done here..." I rotate on my heels, advancing with a decided step toward the gates. I grimace, expecting one of them to stop me on my way out, but nothing comes.

The sister speaks, which makes me laugh and also scream internally.

"Really?" she asks. "Telling her you don't like her hair? How long have you been single? Just get laid."

"Shut up, Maggie."

I'm sweating when I arrive at work, almost late, thanks to those stupid vampires. I receive an interrogative look from my colleague, Maddison—John is starting work when it gets darker—but I ignore her silent question. We get along, barely, but we're not friends. She always resents me a bit for getting away with breaking stuff. It's not my fault if vampires seem to like me.

While I knot my apron that shows off the bar logo, I freeze. My senses are awakened, and with a careful move, I take one, two good sniffs in the air, trying not to look obvious.

Wolves.

Well, that's bad. I haven't met any werewolves. Any smart werewolf knows to avoid New Orleans, even with a tourist pass. I raise my head while quickly walking behind the counter by Maddison's side, and I look around, observing with attention all the early drinkers already present.

I know I'm right; I know this musky smell, especially with the full moon happening in five days. The scent usually gets stronger in males the more we approach the full moon.

I think I spot them. The scent is strongest around three of them. I'm not talented enough to say if they're all werewolves. Let's not forget that, as far as wolves go, I'm not the best hunter. At least I don't know any of them.

I let out a sigh of relief while listening to Maddison ordering me around about what to do next. Why is the witch spell not working on them? Or is it working, but vampires have decided those wolves are not trouble? From what I know, if wolves come through the town, they have to declare themselves, so maybe that explains it. I don't know enough about the administration side of things.

I wish John were here. He's a vampire and has to answer to the king, but maybe those specific wolves are lovely tourists spending their money in town. I don't want to make a scene or have the king ask more questions about why I left the pack. I am not sure how to contact him anyway, so unless John arrives soon, there's no point panicking about it.

But the king has my number, even though I don't have his. I groan. It does not seem very fair, even if the idiot criticized my hair. Of course, I look better as a redhead, but I don't need to hear it now, do I? *Men.*

I spend the rest of my shift carefully avoiding them. I know I have a smell, okay? I'm not dumb. I may not be a werewolf, but I am a shifter with a distinctive scent. They glance at me, but nothing in their look says that they know me, and it's with some relief that they leave after two hours of my shift.

I feel better when they're gone. Funny how trauma works, isn't it?

"John's not coming today; something about getting ready for Halloween night." Maddison interrupts my thoughts, her purple ponytail flying around her as she keeps herself busy, even though today it's quiet.

"Oh, okay. I don't know if I'm working yet on Halloween."

"Aiden and I are. Pretty sure we don't need you."

Bitch.

As I said, we're not friends. Aiden made it clear when I started that he wanted to take me on a date, and Maddison still hasn't forgiven me for it. Apparently, she had been begging for his attention for months.

"Cool," I say, "then I guess I will go to a party."

I probably won't. I'd rather stay home in my sad room and read a book, but she doesn't need to know that. She doesn't answer, and we ignore each other for the rest of the shift. I could have used the generous tips from drunk Halloween partygoers, but it's okay. Fine by me.

CHAPTER 13

MINA

By the end of my shift, my legs feel like jelly, and I reek of bourbon. All I can think about is collapsing onto my mattress and having a good night's rest, hopefully not to be awakened by any vampires.

My street is quiet for once. I'm guessing the girls already went to work, but as I walk toward my building, I'm proven wrong when I see a tall silhouette dressed in red leather.

"Hey, sweetie!" Cherie smiles.

I enjoy seeing a friendly face after this day. She's striding toward me with her feline gait and her impossibly high heels. She seems in a hurry but still stops to give me a quick hug.

"Forgot something?" I ask, raising an eyebrow.

"Condoms." She rolls her eyes. "We're so busy tonight, I can't feel my pussy anymore. Damn, I hate Halloween." I don't have time to answer before she continues. There's no stopping her. "Oh, and by the way—some guy was asking about you. Cute, looking dangerous, screaming red flag."

My heart skips a beat. *Great.* Whoever this is, he's probably gonna interrupt my plan of a peaceful night.

But before I can squeeze out any more information from her, Cherie waves at me and accelerates her clicking heels on the street, adding a wink to her goodbye.

I sigh. A cute guy? It's either Viggo or Gregory trying to drag me back to him. Seriously? You *do* have my number.

I roll my eyes and climb the five flights of stairs to my floor, jumping elegantly between the ones that were still under construction when this building was given up on. The hallway is close to pitch black as usual. The electricians never reached the fifth floor, so the residents combined funds to buy camping LED lights, giving a creepy feel to the whole floor.

I am closer to my room. I can see the purple curtain I suspended there—in lieu of a door—when the hair on the back of my neck rises. It's the smell. Musky, earthy, animalistic. My heart stops mid-beat.

The freaking wolves. I knew it. Of course, they were not just tourists. One could think I was born yesterday.

I freeze, my breath hitching. My brain barely has time to connect the dots before my legs take over.

Nope, not today.

I spin on my heels and run. I race down the stairwell, leaping two steps at a time and jumping over the guardrail. My survival instinct is back, and that is the only thing guiding me. I'm not going back there. Never.

Four floors left. That's all I need. Just make it four floors down, get outside, and—

A low growl echoes from below. My stomach twists. They're intercepting me. One of them must have been smart enough to hide downstairs.

Fine, then. Instead of slowing down, my panic pushes me; it sharpens my movement, and unlike them, I know this place by heart. I jump into a corridor, avoiding random legs spread onto the floor and buckets of vomit. I know exactly which part I'm looking for.

I catch the flicker of moonlight filtering through a window—a window with no glass. Without hesitation, I launch toward it, landing on the scaffolding outside. The metal rattles under my weight, but I don't stop. I climb down, vaulting over bars, leaping between floors with precision. The grunts behind me are getting louder. Those assholes are fast, thanks to the full moon getting closer.

For a split second, I consider flying. Did it once, can do it again. Except that tonight I have a freaking dress with a back zipper and boots that are so tight I usually need to sit to pull them from my feet. I obviously don't have time for this.

Shit, where are my flip-flops when I need them?

Instead, I leap from the second-floor scaffolding to the ground, landing like a cat on the concrete below. My knees absorb most of the impact, but I still wince under the shock. I haven't done any ninja stuff in a while. I gasp for air and I'm ready to take off toward the lighted streets, only to find myself staring at a polished pair of black leather shoes.

Fuck.

I tilt my head up, ready to knock over whoever is reckless enough to stand in my way, when my eyes meet his. A crimson vault filled with interrogation.

The king.

Before I can cry in relief—which, really, I should not—the heavy thud of feet hits the pavement behind me. They jumped too.

My body tenses, and I whirl around, facing the three previous customers. Smoke rises around their bodies, brought by the heat of the approaching full moon. They look at Viggo, and I can see the change in their features as they realize who he is. He's not a figure you easily forget.

And he's faster.

Viggo doesn't hesitate. He moves like lightning; one moment he's standing beside me, the next he's in front of the men, his right hand diving into one of the wolf's chests. The sound of bones crunching echoes through my streets and I turn away.

Within seconds, the two others are lying unconscious in the street, still alive, probably with a purpose. I'm ready to bet they would rather be anywhere else when they wake up.

Viggo cleans off his hand on his leather pants, as if this could wipe the blood dripping from it. Turning to me with a raised eyebrow, he asks, "Rough night?"

I open my mouth to reply something snarly, but I can't help myself and instead embrace his waist with my arms, letting out a strangled cry.

Not long after, I'm sitting on a brown leather couch, the kind you could imagine in those old libraries back in England. It's warm, welcoming, and comforting.

I can't stop looking at the metal hook digging into the ceiling and I truly wonder what it is for. I'm sipping the tea Maggie brought me. I even got a smile from her. I am not into women, but I would happily get in her knickers if she asked me to.

Instead, she seems to believe that I'm very much into her twin's. Yes, it turns out they're twins, which explains a few things, including the way she glances at me, her head cocked to the side, like a cat observing her prey. Her damned luxurious, straight hair falls like a shiny curtain.

My mind keeps jumping back to earlier, and I know those werewolves were here for the damn book I stole six months ago, but thankfully I'm interrupted by Maggie.

"My brother is upset," she says.

I scoff. "He didn't seem that upset when he killed one of the men without a second thought."

She ignores my comment. "He came back with your smell on him. Did you guys cuddle?" She straightens her head, and there's a smug smile on her face.

Rolling my eyes, I take one more sip of my lukewarm tea. "No," I mumble.

"Hmm. Did you want to? I think my brother does."

I scoff into my tea, almost feeling the warm liquid getting out through my nose. "I don't really think your brother is a cuddly bear." I can't stop a chuckle at the thought of this Viking-ass man being all cuddly, dressed in a bear onesie—ideally with nothing under.

"I can be cuddly with you." The voice comes from behind us.

I jolt, while Maggie laughs—I'm sure she knew he was there. Damn vampires!

I almost choke when I see him. His shirt is now covered in blood and... is that... intestines hanging on his shoulder? Ew. I place my tea back on the small table in front of me.

"Not when you're that dirty." I wrinkle my nose.

"This is the blood of your enemy. You should get even cuddlier." The king smirks, and he strides along the room, his long braid swinging in rhythm behind his back. He opens a gigantic wardrobe where he pulls a fresh shirt from. My eyes widen, first because I may very well be in his bedroom, and second because he's taking off his bloody shirt, facing me.

I swallow.

Did I say I was over men? If I did, I lied. You can't be over men when there's a V right in front of you, plunging deep into some tight leather pants.

I stop drooling when I hear chuckles by my side, and I glance at Maggie.

"You look like you just saw some candy," Maggie whispers and winks at me.

I roll my eyes and get my cup of tea back to at least give me something to do with my hands. While I savor it, I follow the king advancing now toward us.

"Maggie, leave us, please."

"Sure," Maggie answers. Before leaving the room, she adds, with an innocent air on her face, "Do I need to ask the witches for an intimacy spell?"

I squeak. What the hell is an intimacy spell? But Viggo just gives her a killer look and thank God she's gone. I mean, I actually like her, but you know. She's not into discretion, that's for sure.

Viggo comes closer and sits next to me. Real close. So close that I can feel the coolness around his skin, and I bet you he is at the front-row seat to hear my racing heartbeat. I can't do that. I can't be with another magical creature who will break my heart so easily.

"I should go home..." I mutter, and I place my empty cup, not wanting to look at him.

"Really?" I can hear the mockery in his voice. It's light, but it's there.

"Yep." I make the 'p' pop.

"You're not going anywhere, Little Wolf."

I look at him, my breath rapid. I know he means it. "Why not? After all, you got the threat under control, didn't you?"

"More could come and seeing how hard they're fighting the torture and the hypnosis, I have a feeling I better keep you under close watch for a little while." He raises one of his hands and follows my jawline, bringing his finger right under my chin. With a gentle push, he tilts my face up a little more.

I can barely breathe; my senses are all confused by his intoxicating presence—not to mention the sexy V imprinted in my brain. This one is going to haunt my dreams for a while.

I swallow and try valiantly to argue. "So, they didn't say why they were here? Could just be a coincidence."

Viggo scoffs.

Yeah, I don't believe myself either.

"Why don't you want to tell me what happened?" He moves his fingers, following the curves of my shoulders, then my arm, reaching my cleavage with an excruciatingly slow touch. "With your pack? If I know better, I can help better."

"You're the king of vampires. I promise, this does not concern you. I was done with the pack, so I ran away."

"Because you were an Omega... I don't blame you. I abhor the wolves' caste system..."

This triggers more curiosity than it should. "Have you met other packs with it? With Omegas?"

I'm genuinely curious. When they first introduced it to us, I thought this was the worst idea in the history of the worst ideas, but is it something common for werewolves? Are we—they—meant to live like this?

"A long, long, time ago." At my interrogative—and begging—look, Viggo chuckles and he stops his excruciating caress to move his hand to my face, cupping my cheeks, bringing me more satisfaction than it should. "When Maggie and I were still mortal, we were living in what is now known as Norway, in the Northern part of it. We were living at peace with every magical creature: witches, werewolves, naiads, and one old vampire lady who was living all by herself."

I already have so many questions, but I don't want to interrupt.

He continues. "My sister and I were both warriors, strong ones. Women could fight, sometimes better than men. More organized, better decisions..."

I laugh. "Yeah, I had this vibe from Maggie."

"The old vampire was a friend of ours. We used to visit her when we were children, and we grew very fond of her. Our mother had passed away, and we only had our father. He was a lovely man but not that much into parenting. So, Brigid brought us the motherly love we were both missing. She was... kind, eager to teach us anything we wanted, any legends she knew of. Once we reached adulthood, many times, she offered us immortal life. Except that she had never created any baby vampires, so she was not sure we would actually become immortal, so we never took the risk, but we enjoyed talking with her about her life."

"How old was she?" I can't help but ask.

"She was born 200 years before our time, not that old."

"Not that old," I mutter, then I say louder, "So...what happened?"

Viggo gives me an expressionless look, his lips in a thin line. "The wolves happened."

I inhale loudly, my eyes wide open.

"They had been grouping, bringing Alphas from every corner of Norway, Finland, Sweden. They had become one, which would not be a problem if there were only one Alpha. By the time we realized it, they had ten."

"Ten Alphas?" Now that's insane. "Why did they group up? They didn't have any actual threat, did they?"

Viggo raises his shoulders. "They didn't. We had petty arguments here and there over territories, but we were always ending on good terms, bringing them gifts from overseas, as they would not be able to travel because of their monthly condition. They just wanted supremacy, and they knew our tribes would stop them. They knew about Brigid and had no doubt she might be the only one able to stop them."

Viggo rises from the couch, and I follow him when he goes to his balcony, overlooking the quiet street below, where jazz plays in the distance. He leans on the metal guardrail and looks at me. "When they attacked us, my tribe tried to fight back, but it was the full moon."

I grimace. Yeah, that's not good.

"They killed everyone, our entire village. They started with men, then hunted down women and children, sparing no one in their path. Maggie and I were still fighting, trying to protect whoever was left. We were trying to move some children away from the battle when we were swiped off our feet, pulled by an incommensurable strength."

I place my hand on his forearm, almost shivering at the touch. I'm such a sucker for sad stories.

"It was Brigid, stealing us away from the battle. Without a word, without giving us a choice, she bit us, both my sister and I, and in a second, she snapped our necks. We woke up a day later. That's how long it takes for a vampire to come back to life. We were... different."

"Why... did she do that? What about the children?"

Viggo turns his full body toward me, moving closer, and holds both sides of my face between his hands. I push into his hands, enjoying the gentle and cold touch.

"She told us we would have died anyway. She was probably right. By condemning the children, she saved us and made sure we took care of the wolves."

"Did you go after the pack?"

"We sure did. We annihilated them. They were not in their wolf shapes anymore, of course, barely stronger than the average mortal. We were starving for blood. For revenge. Since then, every time we hear any start of rumors about the grouping of packs, we make sure to move first. It's not natural. First comes the caste system, then the madness starts."

I bite my lips, my face still hanging in between his hands. "Is... my previous pack still using it? The caste system?"

He chuckles. "Not for now, at least not from what we can see. Unlike what my sister seems to think, I do not slaughter entire packs for the sheer pleasure of it. Unless they give me a good reason to do so, they should be fine. There have been a few movements of the Alphas, though. It seems some have left, others have stayed, but nothing is worrying me at the moment. Your departure seems to have changed things. Or at least I thought so until tonight."

I shiver and move away from his hands, leaning against the balcony. "What did they tell you? The wolves downstairs? I don't even know them."

"But they knew you. They knew who they were looking for. I would love to know why. And how?" His questioning look pierces me.

I hesitate. "I ran away, not exactly on 'good terms.' But I haven't heard from them in six months; I don't see why they would look for me now."

Which is true. Why now? And how the fuck did they find me?

Viggo smiles. I'm sure he knows I'm hiding something, and he's right, but I'm not ready. I don't trust any of them.

"Anyway, Little Wolf. You're not going back to your sad, decrepit building." He dares turn his back on me and walk back into his room.

"Wait... what?" I follow him, ready to give him a slice of my thoughts.

"They knew where you live; you're staying here, you'll be safe."

"I won't. I have a life outside of all of you weird magic people. I'm going back to it. I'm sure they won't come back."

Viggo still appears demurely calm, on the surface at least. "Little Wolf. You'll stay here for as long as I say so, or else I'll burn down your building and anyone who's in there. Don't take my kindness for weakness. Unless you want to tell me what it is you're hiding from me?"

I stay silent for a while after his threat, trying to analyze his cold face, judging how serious he is. I break the silence after deciding he is one hundred percent serious. "Fine, whatever."

CHAPTER 14

MINA

Despite the late hour—someone should tell them normal people actually sleep at night—I am now in the fancy dining room of the king's house, surrounded by three curious faces.

Me staying here? I don't like this idea. Not one bit. Be here in *his* home, where everything feels too intense. Not only is the temptation of him too much to handle, but I don't want him to learn all of my secrets.

Fine, one secret.

I want to sit there and pout like a child, but it's hard to do so when Maggie started talking about how King Viggo was the one who should be held responsible for the extreme leaning of the Pisa tower back during the 13th century.

It's even harder to be grumpy when Viggo is only giving his attention to little ol' me. His eyes barely leave mine, just to sometimes go astray and fix on my lips when I talk, to be followed by this little smirk he does that makes my blood boil and my core warm.

Why am I complaining? The siblings ordered some food from a renowned gastronomy restaurant—according to Maggie—and it may be the best damn chicken I have eaten in my life. The conversations at the dinner flow more naturally than any I had at the pack house. I have to restrain my laugh many times while listening to the banter flowing naturally between the three of them. *Family.* That's what they are.

After an umpteenth laugh escapes me, I glance at Viggo, who is still watching me as if he is trying to decipher me. It's *his* attention that unsettles me. His intense, unreadable gaze and the crazy dance of his veins on his body. I know exactly why I don't like it. I had attention from an Alpha-hole before, and I'm pretty sure my little fragile heart is screaming at me right now to put a stop to whatever *this* is.

I take a deep breath, followed by a full natural yawn. "I think I'm going to bed now... thanks for the dinner."

I stand up, and both Viggo and Gregory do as well, while Maggie remains seated, pouring herself another glass of wine. Blood. Whatever this shimmering crimson drink is.

I glare at the two men. "It's okay. I'm not running away."

I ignore Gregory's chuckles.

Viggo extends his hands. "We were not going to catch you, Little Wolf. From where we're from, from our time, it's rude to stay sitting while a lady stands up."

I stay silent, unsure if I should mention I'm nowhere near a lady and that I highly doubt that Vikings were so gallant. "Okay," I mutter, heading toward the door.

"Do you know where you are going?" asks Viggo, his words immediately stopping me in my tracks.

Obviously not.

I rotate on my heels, trying to hold back my best bitch look. I'm too tired. "No, I don't. Where's my bedroom?"

Viggo smiles and advances toward me until he opens the door, enticing me to follow.

"She wanted to sleep in our coffin," says Gregory behind us, and I hear Maggie laughing. She stops when Viggo turns to her and growls but instead she dramatically places her hand on her forehead.

Viggo rolls his eyes—really not vampire-like—and pushes on my lower back.

We arrive back at the room we were in before, the king's bedroom, and there's a gigantic bouquet sitting on the table. It bears a card with my name on it, written in what must be the most elegant yet masculine writing I have ever witnessed. Too bad I could not carry my fancy pen in my claws when I ran away; I would have let him borrow it.

My heart squeals with excitement but also fear. Why? Seriously, why? Why am I excited by flowers? I glance at the bouquet and brush the petals with care so I don't damage my pretty flowers, and I take a good sniff. I adore the smell of lavender.

I look at Viggo, who eyes me with attention, as if waiting for a proper reaction.

"Why the flowers?" I ask.

"A man doesn't need reasons to bring flowers to a woman," he answers, his face unmoving, as serious as ever. "But if you must know, this is a welcome gift."

Kyle brought me flowers, gifts, and even cheap jewelry. In the end, it still ended up the same. I swallow and pick up the gorgeous vase a servant brings in. I don't want to show how troubled I am by the gift.

While I arrange the flowers, he moves closer. I can feel every movement. Here we go. The whole 'I give you flowers; please suck my dick now' dance is probably starting. His icy hand brushes against my shoulder, and a shiver runs through me.

"Why is this simple gesture upsetting you, my Little Wolf?" he asks.

Before I can find a plausible reason, he shifts, positioning himself in front of me, raising my chin with one of his fingers to force me to look into his eyes. They're a gorgeous crimson color I find fascinating; it seems other vampires enjoy hiding their red eyes with various color contacts, but Viggo does not.

I don't want to look at him, so I direct my eyes to the tattoos on the side of his scalp. I'm pretty sure they're some sort of

Viking design. Their color is faded, but I can guess how intricate they are.

I let out an exaggerated sigh when he, once again, forces my face in another direction, this time catching my chin between two fingers of iron, blocking me so hard that I had to stay there.

"Tell me what I did wrong... do you have any kind of allergies? Or would you have preferred classic red roses?"

The question throws me. It's not what I expected. I blink and pull a fish face, trying to decide if he's mocking me.

His expression is severe, and I can't help but laugh. His brows furrow, his lips tugging down. I wonder if he meant those flowers with no physical expectations.

"I'm just not sure why you... care... so much. I have been through the whole 'playing nice to get what I want from her' thing, and I didn't like it." I pause. "And it didn't end well."

"Right," Viggo says. "'Good terms', was it?" He chuckles slightly at the sight of my rolling eyes.

I freeze when he gets closer to me, placing his forehead against mine, making me feel how cold his body is. My lips part, and I can't control it. This is so simple and also the most intimate act I have done.

"What do you think I want from you, Mina?" he whispers, his lips brushing my skin so lightly it feels like I'm being tickled by butterflies.

"I don't know," I mumble. "I don't like being forced to leave my home..."

"That is for your protection. I know you're not safe there. Do you think I can't protect you?"

"Of course you can." I start pulling myself away from him. "But on one side, I have the wolves coming after me, and then I have you. You're all touchy and caring. I'm scared of when you're gonna ask me to answer to those attentions because when you do, we both know there's no point for me to even try running."

There, I said it. Literally accusing the Bloodsucking King that I'm not expecting much from him.

He observes me carefully, his head tilting. Both he and his sister are starting to get on my nerves with their catlike attitude.

"I think it's tragic that you have been treated so badly that you consider all acts of kindness, of seduction, a personal attack," he says. "I have no interest in getting anything from you that you're not willing to share, Little Wolf. Do I want to fuck you? Yes, I do."

I gasp at those words, pronounced so casually, but he continues.

"Am I going to fuck you because I think I am owed your body? I certainly won't. If you are uncomfortable staying here with me, I can find you a new flat—a safe one. We could place protective spells against wolves on the walls. And against vampires, too."

"I don't have money for that... we could place a spell on my building?" I ask, hopeful. I am already missing my friends and their funny banter, and it has barely been a few hours.

Viggo shakes his head slowly, holding back a laugh. "Your building does not have enough walls to put a spell on it."

Right. He has a point.

"I'll pay for it, for a new safe place for you to stay," he says.

"Against which favors?"

"Nothing."

I scoff and walk in a circle in the room, taking in the rich décor, fabulous textures, ancient artwork, and now the flowers, adding a new smell to the masculine one.

"Okay, maybe a date?" he says. "I'll take you to eat waffles."

"Waff... are you serious?" I never had a waffle, but I know they smell amazing. There's a street shop that sells them, but I could never justify spending my hard-earned tips on a dessert. Or breakfast? I'm not sure which they are.

"Yes." He advances cautiously toward me, catching one of my hands in his, pulling me back closer to him, carefully, as if I would run away. I don't even try to resist. I know he can hear my heartbeat, and I'm sure he knows why.

"Why a waffle? It's really precise."

He chuckles. "I love waffles. They're my favorite food after blood. We have a waffle maker in the kitchen. Maggie makes this killer recipe with blood and whipped cream..."

I let out a shocked laugh. "I'd rather have chocolate on mine. When was the last time you went on a waffle date?" I ask, watching him under my eyelashes, and I move my hand slowly onto his chest. It is a weird feeling to be terrified of something yet run for it.

"A long time. I don't need to beg women for waffle dates, usually. Women always want to sleep with me, often with no dates or gifts," he says with a funny, contrite look on his face.

"One date and one waffle are not gonna get you that. I can tell you right now." I scoff, but leave my hand on his hard chest, enjoying the touch more than I should, wishing I would be brave enough to slip my hands between the buttons of his shirt.

"I know." Viggo moves closer. He places one of his hands to rest on my own, slowly bringing it to his mouth, letting me get a glimpse of quite pointy teeth.

"Fine. Tomorrow after my shift? I finish at five, perfect for a snack time!" I say, then add without thinking, "Are you planning to eat me?" After all, that's a fair question; those fangs of his are scary.

"No, I'm planning to eat the waffle… unless you let me have a taste. I have been dreaming of the day I would finally sink my fangs into your perfect skin."

"Not funny."

He laughs and moves his arms around my waist, pulling me closer to him, making me gasp. "I'm immortal, little wolf, and a very patient man when I yearn for something. I'm not sure why or by which miracle you are still a virgin, but I'm ready to wait. But for this, you need to allow me to seduce you. Slowly, tenderly, the same way I'm planning to make love to you one of those days."

I feel my mouth opening and closing, like I'm a goldfish in a bowl. Viggo raises a brow.

"How the heck do you all know I'm still a virgin?" I blurt out, trying to forget his last sentence, which is affecting my lower parts more than I would have expected.

This time, a loud laugh comes out of him. "Please. Your smell is quite obvious." He pulls me further, nudging his head toward the king bed sitting in the room. "Come now, get to bed."

I stop. "In here? In your room?" *In his bed?*

"Of course. It's easier to protect you this way." His fangs grow to an impressive length, shining under the lamplight.

I want to protest, thinking about all my good resolutions. But then, how bad can it be to get cuddly with the vampire king? The huge bed with a soft bordeaux-colored comforter is calling my name right now, and I deserve a good night's sleep.

CHAPTER 15

MINA

I WAKE UP SLOWLY, feeling a weird mix of warmth and cold pressing against my back. A firm, strong body molds to perfection against my curves. The vampire king is spooning me. Right.

I am enjoying this more than I should.

That realization slaps me in the face; my eyes snap open when just a few seconds earlier I was ready to go back to sleep. The room is still dark. The heavy curtains hanging at the windows obscure the sunlight. I have a shift today at one, and I can't afford to miss it, seeing that I'm not working on one of the biggest nights of the year. My alarm didn't wake me up yet, so at least I can assume I'm not late. Added to the curtains are metallic blinds; only the best to protect the king from the deadly sun. It's dark here, but the time is just a mess in this house anyway—these people live by night after all. I grimace. That probably means I can forget about a coffee for my breakfast and go straight for a beer.

Yuck, no, I need coffee.

I shift carefully, glancing back. Viggo looks dead, which, well... he is. I hold my breath for a second, half-expecting him to jump on me, fangs out and ready for his morning snack. But no. Just stillness. I observe him for a few seconds, enjoying the quiet.

His skin is the same translucent color as usual, but when he sleeps, the purple veins under it are almost shining, with colors and glows moving along. It's kind of pretty, but a tad creepy.

I have no idea what time vampires wake up, so I decide to hunt for coffee and slip out of bed in silence, padding toward his luxurious bathroom, which I had a quick preview of yesterday. I throw a quick splash of cold water on my face, but I don't dare check his drawers to find a comb for my hair. Maybe he doesn't need one. His braid is so pretty that someone must be doing it for him. My thoughts wander quickly to the king and his long, gorgeous hair flying around. I wonder what he would look like without a braid.

I leave the bedroom as quietly as I can, glancing at the king still asleep and hugging my pillow.

Really? I should take a picture.

I hold back a giggle and head downstairs, where, thank God, I can smell actual coffee. The stairs and corridors have no natural light. This entire place seems to have been amended to suit vampires. Thankfully, the amount of various ceiling lights, chandeliers, and even some floor lighting gives the entire place a warm but bright ambiance, straight from any vampire movie.

Entering the same dining room from yesterday, I can't help but widen my eyes. The table is dressed as if we were going to the fanciest restaurant in Paris, silver shining under the lights and porcelain plates of every shape imaginable. Someone in this house is not afraid of my skills at breaking things.

More importantly, there's a buffet taking up the entire length of the wall with actual breakfast-tolerated food.

Trying not to drool on the food, I spot Maggie, already sipping from a cup and looking my way with an air far too smug for so early in the... whatever time it is.

"How many people are living in this house?" I ask her, picking a plate on the table and helping myself, more than generously, to any sweet pastry I can spot.

"Only us four are, with you now."

The way she said 'us' makes warmth pool in my stomach.

I raise my head and pick up one more croissant. "Are you guys ogres or something?"

"No. My brother just wasn't sure what you wanted to eat in the morning. So, he ordered everything he could think of."

I stop everything I'm doing. You could buy me all the flowers in the world, and I might not give you the time of day. But give me food? I would do anything you ask.

Smart vampire.

I sigh, and don't bother trying to control my heartbeat. I know from Maggie's mousy look that she notices it. That's when I spot what the gorgeous brunette is stirring in her coffee. Instead of cream, deep red swirls in. Who am I to judge? They need blood, after all.

"So, you're still here," Maggie says, taking a casual sip. "What happened to the 'I'm a strong independent woman who doesn't want to cuddle in your big muscular arms' act?" She said those words in a high-pitched fake voice; I'm guessing, in a poor attempt at imitating me.

"Shut up," I grumble, hesitating only a second before dropping into the seat beside her.

Maggie doesn't look like a terrifying vampire now. I mean, if you forget the blood in her coffee, her white skin, and those purple veins on her body. She is dressed in white, again, but this time it's a timeless dress, showing off a square cleavage that suits her to perfection. She looks absurdly normal, like an important CEO heading for a meeting, reading her newspaper. I glance at it, expecting something dull, like stock actions or war, but the bold, dramatic headlines make me blink a few times. *"Are you more into vampires, werewolves, or mermen? Take our quiz now to find out your next bang!"*

"Is that... a supernatural gossip newspaper?" I blurt, resisting the urge to snatch it from Maggie. I have never heard of such a thing. Werewolves are backward sometimes. Also, are mermaids an actual thing? I have so many questions. I remember the king mentioning naiads from his youth, so I guess I should not be surprised. I wonder how many creatures I'm still to discover.

"Sure is." Maggie smirks. "Mostly run by vampires. Used to be boring as hell, just rich vamps talking about other rich vampires. Lately, it's gotten juicy, especially since one of my best friends is in charge of it. Lots of scandals. Lots of sex."

I swallow my coffee with difficulty. I don't like the way Maggie is looking at me.

"Speaking of which…" She starts to speak.

I cut in quickly, barely holding back a wince. "Your brother and I are *not* lovers." We were spooning, that's all. Spooning is allowed.

Maggie rolls her eyes. "I know, which is why I was going to invite you to a party tomorrow night. Halloween."

I love Halloween. But—"I have work." Yep, it's a blatant lie.

"I'll ask John; he owes me a few favors." She shrugs her shoulders as if this is nothing. She probably never had to get an actual job in her life, except when she was busy raiding neighborhood villages.

I grimace. Of course, she would know my boss. "I'm not sure that's the best idea."

Does Viggo want me there? I am not sure I want to see him getting all touchy with other women on the sexiest night of the year.

"You'll be safe, don't worry."

"I'm not sure Viggo wants me there," I mutter. "And honestly? This is only temporary; I don't want people getting ideas about me, like I'm his new pet or something."

"Is that what you think I want of you?"

I flinch. Of course, he is awake now. And of course, he is right behind me, staring with that quiet intensity that he never seems to get rid of.

"Sorry... I meant a pet you can fuck and control."

Oh, no. I'm back to being a whiny idiot. Coffee. I need more coffee.

Maggie laughs. Viggo does not.

In a blink, he is on me, lifting me up effortlessly and throwing me over his shoulder. Coffee followed by a ruthless carry? Not the best combo.

"Hey! Put me down, you—"

"If I wanted to fuck you," he growls, his voice low and dangerous, "I would have already. I would have fed on you, had you screaming my name, and made sure you never left this house or my bed a virgin. You need to accept that not every man you meet wants to hurt you. I thought we were past that. Did you even listen to our conversation yesterday?"

He puts me back down on the floor of his bedroom. I can't believe I got carried back here before even finishing my breakfast. My breath is barely catching up.

"You're scaring me right now," I murmur in a raspy breath.

"Good, at least one of your fears is justified."

Before I can snap back, a voice interrupts the tension in the room, in a language I don't recognize.

Gregory stands in the doorway. His usual smug look on his face is mixed with an unimpressed look. Whatever he said, it darkened Viggo's expression. I won't lie, I'm glad his attention and anger are redirected to someone else.

He sighs, addressing me. "Go pack your things back home. Take Maggie with you."

I blink. "What?"

"If you don't, I'll burn down the building where your friends live."

"You wouldn't—"

He cuts me off. "It's not safe for you out there, and until I fully understand why, or until you tell me why, you're under my protection. Because you just pissed me off first thing in the morning, you're staying in this house. With me."

I'm not the only one who needs a coffee before a civilized conversation.

He walks toward the door and turns, a smirk on his lips. "And if you don't listen, I'll show you exactly what the hook in this room that seems to intrigue you is for."

I gasp and look at the hook. Is it for punishing people or something? Why is it in his room, though?

The king leaves, and I am alone, stress taking over. I don't want him to be angry at me, not because I fear him, but because I don't want it. I grab a cushion and throw it onto the bed. That's not that impactful, but it still feels good. Kyle and his little Alpha friends fucked me up. I can't even accept help from a sexy-ass vampire king. How bad could it be to sleep in a nice bed and have unlimited breakfast every day?

CHAPTER 16

VIGGO

I'M STILL HOLDING BACK my rage, clenching my fist. My blood flows faster under my skin; it always does when I go through intense feelings. The older I get, the more noticeable my veins become. Thankfully, this is New Orleans. Nobody cares about a weird six-foot-five, weird-looking guy.

Mina is driving me insane. For once, I care about a woman, and the woman could not care less about my help.

I know it all started at her previous pack. One does not become an Omega and enjoy it. Maybe my sister is right, and I should slaughter all of them, send a message to any werewolves thinking about grouping forces. Make a statement. I would bring their bleeding heads and their hearts, still beating in my hands, to Mina and invite her to bathe in their blood, vowing my will to protect her.

She'll probably still won't get the message.

There were children among the pack, and since the night we became vampires, we promised ourselves we would never let a child get hurt on our watch, even though experience taught us that when you leave children alive behind, they always come for revenge.

I fly down the narrow stairs leading to our basement, my footsteps echoing on the stone. Initially, it was a bourbon-making basement. Now, I've made it into a prison. Only five cells, with the strict minimum inside. I rarely keep prisoners. Either you're guilty, or you're not.

I sigh when I spot the dead body hanging from the window's bars, the only bulb in the room flickering above him. Gregory didn't lie. One of the werewolves I brought back from Mina's attack killed himself. The man took his belt out and hanged himself using the bars at the tiny window. He preferred death to betraying his Alpha.

I observe the body in silence.

This is the second sign that something bad is coming.

First, they regroup.

Then, the caste system.

Third, they'd rather die. They're linked to their Alpha—or Alphas—so hard they will always choose death.

"Who interrogated him?" I ask.

"Me." Gregory scowls. "And I didn't even start hurting him yet. I swear."

He doesn't need to swear. I have entrusted my sister's life in his hands after all.

"I know. Did he say anything at all?"

Gregory shakes his head, advancing toward me and giving me a piece of paper, where a neat, feminine writing gives an address. Mina's address. "It was in his pocket."

I growl. They're indeed looking for her. I knew it. This is more than just an Omega leaving a pack. Even if sometimes an Omega owes money to the pack, they would never go as far as invading a vampire city just to find her, unless they have definitely lost their mind. Wolves are so confusing with the way they do things.

"How do you wanna play it?" asks Gregory.

I turn to him, a slight interrogation in my eyes.

"I mean... do we announce that he's dead? Or do we just act as if nothing happened?"

It takes me two seconds to make my decision, and with a wry smile, I glance at my friend. "Group him and the other wolves from yesterday, cut their heads, and send them back to Kyle in a nice package. Werewolves are not allowed in the city unless they're tourists or validated by one of us first. That's the rule."

"That's the rule." Gregory smirks.

I head back to my bedroom, hoping to solve the unresolved conflict with my Little Wolf.

"What about Mina?" asks Gregory. "Should I mention her? Like... digging the knife a tad or something?"

I look at him. "You want to upset them, don't you?"

He laughs. "Yeah. I don't like those little hairy shits. How about I just add the piece of paper with the address, and mention something like 'please forward courier or werewolves assassins to 54A Bourbon street?'"

I try hard to hold back a smile. Gregory always had a gift for practical jokes; it compensates for my pragmatic side.

MINA

I have been walking back and forth in his bedroom for longer than I want to. I still have time before my shift, but I need to talk to Viggo first. I hate feeling like we left things unresolved.

Finally, he returns, and there's a slight sign of relief on his face as he spots me. He stands there without a word, his arms crossed behind his back.

"What's happening?" I ask.

"The last wolf alive from yesterday killed himself."

My eyes widen. This sounds like quite a drastic solution. "Did he say anything about why he was here?" My voice shakes, my thoughts flying toward the book I stole six months ago. Are they here for it?

"Unfortunately, not a word." Viggo advances slowly. "Gregory is preparing a... gift... for your ex-Alpha."

"A gift? That asshole does not deserve a gift." Oops. I said it.

Viggo laughs, and my heartbeat rises to the sound, so beautiful, so natural. I don't move when he gets closer to me, and I barely flinch when he catches my waist, bringing my body closer to his. I'm just happy he doesn't seem angry at me anymore.

"Don't worry, my Little Wolf, this is not a gift he's going to enjoy," he whispers, his face closer to mine, his breath reaching me, his lips so close I could kiss him.

"What... do you mean?"

"A few heads and guts in a box. A statement. Gregory loves those."

He brushes my cheeks with his nose, heading toward my ear, and smells me like we are at the florist and I'm a bouquet. The sensation makes me shiver, and I hold back a whimper, feeling a fire waking up in me that I would very much rather stay stifled. I try to catch his gaze, trying to understand, to feel what's happening here between us.

"Your pack will know they're not welcome here, and they will know you're under my protection."

I gasp. Okay, that's a big step. Kyle is *not* gonna like that. His little whore is not accessible even for a basic slaughter? Ouch.

"This way, when you're ready to tell me the full story, it will be easier for me to adapt."

His crimson eyes bore into me, so intense, as if burning, and there is barely any space left between our bodies. My breath hitches with desire—something I thought I would not feel for a *long* time. He glances at my lips, and I lick them. Then, on an impulse, I jump.

I jump straight to his lips, grabbing him by the neck and pulling him down toward me, not thinking about consequences or his reactions. I just want him. I want to feel him. I want to be devoured by him.

His reaction is immediate, and he holds my face between both hands, keeping me pinned to his face, licking my lips, nibbling on them, and enticing a whimper from me. I grab his shoulders and accentuate our kiss, never letting go of him; this must be the best kiss in the history of best kisses. I want more. I find myself wishing we were naked so I could grind on him until I reach my long-awaited pleasure.

"Please do it." Viggo stops the kiss to whisper to me, still holding my face, his gaze locked on me.

I gasp. "Wait... how?"

"Sorry, when I have a... close... interaction with someone, sometimes I can hear them. I can feel you. Your mind was not discreet about this." He chuckles. Asshole.

I try to push him away, self-conscious of how naughty I must have sounded.

"Don't be ashamed, my Little Wolf; you have no idea how much I desire you. As I told you before…" He grabs me and lifts me without an ounce of effort to sit me around his waist, my legs hanging over his back. In a few steps, he drops onto the leather couch, and his hands are climbing my thighs. When his hands reach the hem of my dress, he looks at me, as if waiting for instructions. "I'm very patient," he says, gently rubbing my skin, creating a new fire.

I bite my lips and close my eyes, enjoying the caress. I never got a soft touch when I was with Kyle. It was always rough, gone in a blink because of how furious he was with my lack of cooperation. Viggo holds my neck and brings me toward his lips.

"If you want to grind yourself on me until you climax, I'm fine with it. I would love to witness it. But if you're not ready, I am still happy to spend the next hour kissing you."

I open my eyes to look at him, taking a deep breath and lifting my dress until it goes above my waist, clenching it in one of my fists while I use my other hand to keep my balance on him.

Then I grind. I move my body on him, keeping my clit right on the bulge of his jeans, feeling the rough fabric against my silk panties. I groan. The pleasure is immediate. I haven't been touched in so long, not even just playing with myself. The rubbing is incredible. The feeling of his hands holding my ass and guiding my rhythm drives me insane. The intensity of his gaze on me is incomparable.

I moan, loud, not caring for a minute about who could hear us. "You're so hard." It's a stupid thing to say but also quite matter-of-fact.

"You make me hard, Mina. I can't wait to taste you."

He grabs both my arms in a swift movement and blocks them behind my back with one hand. I whimper, feeling like a prisoner, my cheeks burning. My panties are probably in an indescribable mess, but I continue moving, enjoying every second of it.

He glances at my cunt, and with a naughty smile, he moves his free hand toward it.

I gasp.

"Is this okay?" he asks, pulling my panties to the side. I know my pussy is on full display, probably red and glistening with my juice, with my clit throbbing.

I nod, barely able to breathe.

"Say it, Mina." He orders.

"It's okay," I whisper, grinding harder, this time feeling the rough jeans on my clit. The pain becomes one with my pleasure, and my moans grow louder.

"By Odin, you have the prettiest, juiciest cunt I have ever seen in my life." He grunts, tightening his hold on my arms, which are still stuck behind my back.

Those words make me whine, accelerating my pace.

"I want to taste you, to bite you, to play with this pretty pink nub of yours." His hands clench. "Do you remember the first day we met? I could smell your blood from any distance... I was barely able to contain myself, wishing I could ravage you right there, tasting your pussy and the blood escaping from it, making you scream my name while your entire pack watched in agony."

It's with those words that I finally come, and I come hard. My head falls back, and every inch of my body contracts under the strength of my orgasm. I'm coming all over him. *Fuck.*

I move around, stuttering various apologies, but he holds me back and growls. *Growls.*

"Don't you dare say sorry for having you climax this way? This is the most exciting thing I have seen. And actually..." He catches me under my butt and, without more foreplay, he lays me down on the couch.

My weak complaints go unheard. My body is still shaking from pleasure, and I let him have his way, but I'm ready to say no if I see an inch of his dick.

He licks two of his fingers and slowly bends over me, not looking away. I feel the stretch. One finger first, gently, so gentle. I relax and spread my legs to give him better access. He brushes the pad of his finger against the top of my wall, and I moan under the nice pressure. Viggo smiles and, after a few seconds, inserts his second finger. I am so drenched that I barely feel the stretch. I moan when his fingers softly curl and hit what I know is my G-spot.

I have heard about it, I have read about it, but I have definitely never found it.

My moans are getting out of this world when Viggo finally starts moving. Faster, stronger, both his fingers inside me, hitting that perfect spot, driving me to the edge of my pleasure. I hold my legs, and I am spread wide on the couch, not caring about how dirty this is going to get.

I whimper. "Harder, please. Harder!"

He growls again, fingering me with so much strength that I'm ready to have my eyes pop out of my head, until it comes. Another orgasm, even more powerful than the first one. My moan gets louder, and my panting gets closer.

"Come for me, Mina... come for me..." He groans, and one of his hands brushes lightly against my breast, which is still covered by my dress.

And I do. Pulling my legs wider, I come hard and wet, spraying all over him. He growls under his breath while he looks with fascination at my juices all over his hands and his couch. I lay my legs down and look at him, still sitting between my legs. His veins are doing this funny dance, and it seems the entire purple cover is concentrated in a very specific part of his anatomy. I bite my lips to hold my smile.

"Don't make fun of me, Little Wolf. You're driving me insane."

He opens his fly, and I feel a slight excitement, quickly overshadowed by panic. He immediately calms me down. "Don't worry, you don't have to do anything. I just want to come on you, the same way you came on me."

I nod, with a tad too much enthusiasm, and I watch him intensely as he takes his dick out—a big, veiny, shiny one. This is much bigger than Kyle's. If I see him again, I'll make sure he knows.

I'm panting when he starts stroking himself with rage. He groans under the pressure of his hand. I make my decision quickly.

"Let me touch you," I murmur, catching his thick length in my hand, shyly stroking him.

He moves one of his hands to the side of my face, and I can't help but kiss his palm. Quickly, he's panting as much as I was and squirming under my touch, begging me to go harder, which he doesn't need to beg me for too long about.

"Tell me when you're coming, tell me." I beg him and accelerate my hand while trying to undo the top of my dress with my other hand.

The king chuckles. "Not sure what your plan is, but I like it." In one move, he rips off my dress, under my protest, and holds one of my tits in his hands, playing with my hard nipple.

"You said you wanted to come on me," I say. When I feel him struggling in my hand, I bend over, offering him my breast, playing with one of my nipples, while never letting go of his gaze. The reaction is fast and intense, and quickly I am covered with his cum, playing with it, spreading it all over my tits while I keep my gaze on him.

Viggo sighs and closes his eyes, happy and without a word, brings me closer to him, hugging me. He's such a hugger.

CHAPTER 17

MINA

Tʜᴇ sᴏᴜɴᴅ ᴏғ ᴍʏ laughter reaches my ear, and I don't recognize myself. *Jeez, girl, get a grip.*

Here I am, playfully fighting the terrifying king of vampires to let me get out of the bathroom without him catching me. Who would have thought that the oldest being on Earth was like a puppy? After our intense, intimate session, we go to the bathroom, where, against my protest, the king draws me a bath. Makes *us* a bath. We spend an hour cuddling in warm water, touching and caressing each other like shy lovers. This must be the best time I've ever had with a man by far.

I couldn't help myself but to hide my mark, this hatred branding my previous pack did on my skin, and I don't think

Viggo saw it. He was just happy I would lie against him, making sure my shoulder stayed in contact with his skin.

I hate myself for loving this so much, for enjoying my time with him. Less than twenty-four hours ago, I was quite determined about avoiding the whole supernatural world. What the heck am I doing? At the same time as this sneaky thought reaches my mind, I let my eyes wander over him. He is drying himself, as if this is the most natural thing in the world, not caring about hiding any part of his body. I bite my lips at the sight of his half-hardened penis, still covered in purple veins. I *never* felt this way with Kyle; this is not comparable in any way. If Kyle had treated me like this, I may have happily given myself to him. But with Viggo? I feel... safe. Which is a weird feeling considering he's probably the most dangerous creature on the planet.

I hide a smile while I steal another look toward him, and I go to get dressed. Oh, right. I have no clothes. I pick up my destroyed dress from the floor and throw it at him, still half dressed. "You ruined one of my only dresses!"

Viggo catches it and brings it to his nose, resulting in my breath speeding up.

He raises a provocative eyebrow. "You asked for it, little wolf."

I pout, tightening the towel over my body. "Well, I have nothing to wear now... and I am supposed to go to work." I check the fancy clock on the wall. "Oh, my God, I have to go *now!*"

I panic, looking frantically for my panties while Viggo laughs behind my back.

I make it to my shift, but not without difficulties. I had to borrow an outfit for Maggie, so I am now dressed in a gorgeous white satin skirt and a white, deep-V shirt. Considering that I work in a bar and have a limited set of skills, wearing all white is calling for trouble. I hope Maggie doesn't expect to get these clothes back.

I glare at the man sitting in a dark corner of the bar, carefully avoiding the direct sunlight. Of course, I was not allowed to come in here on my own, so here's poor Gregory, acting as bodyguard despite the sun still shining bright.

I would give anything to witness John's widened eyes again when I arrived, dressed in my fancy clothes. He was already starting to give me a disappointed look about my lateness, then he saw Gregory following me, with a cap pulled down on his face, grumbling about the sun. Thankfully, Gregory mentioned that I was late because I had 'important' business with the king, which probably saved me from getting an earful.

After bringing drinks to the few customers, I turn to John. "How come you're here so early?"

He sighs. "Maddison called in sick today, and Aiden could not start before two. He should be here soon. I am going back to bed as soon as he arrives."

I hold back my chuckle and continue my fascinating task—slicing lemons. Exciting, indeed.

Five minutes later, Aiden joins us. His hair is artfully messy, and his blue eyes brighten when he sees me. He lets his eyes roam over my body without shame. "Hey, girl, you're looking great today. That's a new look."

I can only give him a strained smile, still trying to adjust to my new clothes, which are too white and fancy for my taste. I like Aiden. Unlike Maddison, he doesn't treat me like shit, but his whole puppy attitude, waiting to get a treat, tends to push my buttons. I do what any smart woman would: I'm trying to send as few signals as I can.

We wave to John when he finally leaves through the back door, relief showing on his face about going back to the darkness. Instantly, Aiden is onto me, making small talk. Why is this place so empty all of a sudden? I sure wish we had some customers to take care of, but Gregory is one of five clients today, and he has been sipping on the same damn glass of bourbon for the past hour.

"So, what are you doing for Halloween?" he asks, leaning casually on the counter, his arms crossed. His gaze drops quickly to my cleavage before snapping back up like nothing happened.

I ignore it; men are men, after all. "Well, I'm not working. I was going to chill, but it seems there's a party I am invited to."

"Oh, that sounds cool. Maybe I'll join after my shift!"

I freeze, blinking at him, trying to stop my eyebrows from rising to the ceiling. "I'm... pretty sure it's by invitation only."

I don't want to be responsible for his probable death if he were to step foot in a vampire party. I glance at Gregory. He observes us, with his elbows on the table, chin resting in his hands like a teenage girl soaking up gossip. I wince when he pulls his phone and takes a picture of me.

Annoying vampire.

I almost forget to pay attention to Aiden's babbling about Halloween until I hear the word 'date.' I rotate my head back to him. "Date *what* now?"

"A date? You and me? We could go to the party together..." He has subtly moved closer to me.

I take one step back, not-so-subtly. I need my space. Unless it's Viggo letting me grind on him, then it's fine. I'm about to answer something polite but clear when the entrance door opens with a bang, scaring me.

The King of Vampires himself swooshes in, his jaws more tense than I have ever seen before, his eyes red like a blaze. He comes straight to the counter with an unnatural speed. Both Aiden and I look at him, Aiden with curiosity and me with way too much trepidation.

Viggo orders. "Old Rip. Straight."

I don't say a word but quickly pour a glass of the desired drink, my heart racing in my chest.

"Here you go," I mutter, sliding the glass to him, giving him a silent signal message through my eyes.

Viggo is having none of it. He remains, unmoving, keeping his cold look on my colleague. Then, in slow motion, he picks up his glass and advances toward Gregory's spot. I don't even want to look at Gregory; I know he is probably laughing his ass off.

Aiden curiously watches Viggo walk away, and then, as if deciding that crazy guys are not his problem, he returns to the attack about the date. The fool.

"Sooo, about tomorrow night? Drop your party and wait for me? I have been meaning to—"

Viggo interrupts him with no ceremony. "She's busy." His back is to us, his hands gripping the counter. His veins dance around in a worrying way.

"Am I?" I ask, lifting a brow.

"Yes."

"Well, what am I busy doing?" I rotate my body to face Viggo, leaning onto the counter.

He glares at me, stretching his hands to twirl one of my curls around his finger. "Me. You're busy doing *me*."

I scoff and slap his wrist. He pulls back with a satisfying smug smile on his lovely lips. Aiden mumbles something about cleaning glasses, and when I look, he's at the opposite side of the bar.

I give Viggo my most unimpressed look. "You didn't need to be rude," I whisper. "I am not interested in him; he's just trying his luck."

"I don't like other men trying their luck, Little Wolf. Besides, this guy has fucked all of his colleagues; he probably intends on treating you like an old sock."

I roll my eyes. "And? You and I are not a couple."

Viggo chuckles darkly. "You're right, we're not, but we're going on a date today. I would think it's polite not to agree to go somewhere else with another guy. Especially with one so boring."

"I was not going to." I stand back, grumpy. "I have to work; go do your vampire stuff somewhere else. I'll see you after."

Of course, he takes a seat beside Gregory, never letting go of me for the next three hours.

CHAPTER 18

VIGGO

I HAVE BEEN OBSERVING Mina for the past hours, enjoying how her skirt suits her round ass and how the fabric pulls when she bends over, showing the lace of the panties she's wearing. I can tell she's not happy with my behavior, but I have no doubt I can make her forgive me. Gregory has given up accompanying me in my stalking and left the bar a while ago.

I get up when the clock shows five and go to Mina, patiently waiting for her. She throws me a look. I have to hold back my laugh as she mutters a goodbye to the asshole who thought he could score a date with my Mina.

"You'd better buy me two waffles with extra chocolate," she says, heading to the door while ignoring my offered arm.

I chuckle. "Anything you want, Little Wolf."

We step out, and she glances to the sky, a concerned look on her gorgeous face. "Looks like it's gonna rain!"

"It's fine, we're not going far." I extend my arm again to her.

She gives me a slight pout but finally accepts it, her warm fingers closing on my skin.

As predicted, it starts raining, and we find ourselves running in the fresh rain. We don't go far before I pull Mina to safety under a hiding corner. Her white dress clings to her skin, nearly translucent. Even though I already knew she was not wearing a bra today, I divert my eyes toward her perky tits, pushing through the fabric, tempting me.

"Eyes on my eyes," she dares to say, interrupting my thoughts of all those things I'm planning to do to her as soon as she lets me.

"I can't. I should teach you a lesson for driving me crazy today."

She scoffs, squirming under my gaze as I step closer, blocking her from escaping.

"What kind of lesson?" she asks.

A shriek escapes her as I grab her arms and block them above her head with a hand, while my other hand brushes her face. My body is so close to her that I know she can feel how much I desire her. She still gasps when I push my hips against her, forcing her to look at me.

I caress her cheeks, mouth, and lips, playing with them with my thumb. With satisfaction, I see her licking her lips. Her breath is already speeding up, her heartbeat all over the place. I go lower, following the tender skin around her collarbone, until I finally reach the soft curve of her tit.

"Viggo..." She whines, squirming her body under my touch, looking around frantically as the crowd runs happily under the heavy rain, not paying attention to our little corner of paradise.

I move my hand to one of her nipples, rubbing it between my fingers, instantly obtaining a loud moan from her.

"My favorite noise," I whisper.

"Please—stop."

I let go of her arms, allowing her to push me if she wants to, but continue my sweet torture on her body. "Are you sure, Mina? This seems to please you." I give a strong squeeze to her perky nipple, resulting in a strangled whine as an answer. I can't help but smile as I move lower, lifting the hem of her skirt.

"Viggo!" She gasps, still glancing toward the now-empty street, filled with water instead of drunk tourists.

"Tell me, Mina, how wet are you right now?" I whisper into her ear, nibbling on her lobe, enjoying the shivers running through her.

"I'm not wet," she answers, her eyes bright, her pulse faster than ever.

"Really?" I mock, and I slowly move my hand below her skirt, lifting the soft fabric to reach her warm core. Despite her complaints, I touch her through her panties. Soaked. As predicted. I chuckle, and she gives me a tap on the chest, pouting grumpily.

I block her hands behind her back this time, holding her even closer to me, her back arched against the stone. My other hand goes straight for her pussy, following her slit, feeling the wetness through the fabric. I rub up and down until I stop on her little nub that I can feel through the laces. Her moan intensifies as I circle it, and she whimpers when I move aside the fabric, brushing her skin, entering her slowly.

"Looks quite wet to me." My voice is raspy, and I accelerate my back and forth inside of her, feeling her tight cunt clenching around my finger.

"It's the rain," Mina mutters, her hips dancing against my hand.

I laugh aloud. "Really?" I bring my fingers to my mouth, sucking on my digits. "Doesn't taste like rain to me."

Mina licks her lips; her eyes are fixated on my hand.

I chuckle and bring it to her red lips, pulling her lower lip with my thumb, spreading her juice over it. "Still tastes like the rain, Little Wolf?"

Mina shakes her head weakly, keeping my fingers in her mouth.

"Good. Next time this guy asks, don't hesitate. I may be patient, but I don't share." I pull my fingers from her mouth and go lower, moving my hand back up toward her pussy. "And this sweet little pussy of yours"—I insert two of my fingers, sliding nicely inside her cunt, while I listen to her moans—"is mine."

She gets louder, and I move my other hand to her mouth, stopping her from screaming, her whimpers half hidden by the loud noise of the rain around us. As I accelerate my movement, Mina's eyes go to heaven, and I can hear her heartbeat ready to explode. She moves her hand on my hand, clenching it while she starts riding her climax.

"That's good, come for me, Little Wolf, learn your lesson."

Her hips move in rhythm with my hands, and she looks like she is out of this world, already in her own paradise. As she finally comes, her tight pussy clenches on my fingers. Her juice runs down my hands, and her legs shatter under the strength of her orgasm.

I hold her face between my hands, not caring about spreading her delicious orgasm on her skin. "Next time you defy me, Little Wolf. You will have a taste of the hook."

CHAPTER 19

MINA

WE COME BACK DRENCHED from our adventure in the street. After my many protests, Viggo agrees to let us return home instead of heading out for our date. While I draw myself another bath, he orders those famous waffles, accompanied by some sparkling wine. We sit in his gigantic bath for a while, eating waffles and drinking wine, talking. Like, actual *talks*. I could get used to this. Of course, there are a few brushes of our hands, soft caresses, and promises of much pleasure while doing so.

When we finally get out, I run away from him and his grabby hands, which gives me a sense of deja vu, and I look through the few clothes Maggie left for me. We are supposed to pick up my stuff and go shopping for Halloween.

I squeal when Viggo playfully catches me out of nowhere, grabbing my ass and turning me to face him.

"No!" I laugh, pushing him while I run away with my towel. "I'm supposed to go shopping with your sister—who has been waiting for me for hours." I sure hope she is more patient than she looks.

He raises an eyebrow. "Shopping? Did she convince you to redo your entire wardrobe?"

I scoff. What's wrong with my wardrobe? "No, she invited me to the Halloween party tomorrow night, remember?"

Viggo straightens up and slowly puts his new shirt on, which makes me sad. I do enjoy looking at his V. "Right. That's what you were talking about earlier. I'm not sure how much of you in a sexy Catwoman outfit I can handle, Mina."

He moves closer to me, his eyes bright red and his fangs growing to a worrying length.

I scream and grab a cushion on the couch to throw it at his face. "I am not planning to be Catwoman; it's too cliché."

"Good. Whatever it is, I will enjoy taking it off you later. I still have more of you to discover." While saying so, he manages to reach me, catching my chin in his fingers and raising my face to meet his burning eyes.

Gosh. I could grind on him all over again and be perfectly happy.

Oh shit.

"Did you hear that?" I mutter, holding onto my towel.

His voice is raspy and barely a whisper. "Yes."

"Right. Of course, you did. I should get dressed now."

"Yes, you should. I'll go look for Maggie."

I take a deep breath while he gets out of the room, watching his muscular back as he walks. What am I getting into?

I have to hold back some tears when I wave goodbye to my friends. Ms. Marble, Cherie, and Anya. They all scream various goodbyes, mixed with obscene gestures. I may have made a mistake telling them I may have found someone.

Immediately, they asked me if he was a sugar daddy, and stupid Maggie answered, "He's not a sugar daddy; he's a king." Her voice carried all the seriousness of a millennial vampire who dresses in only one color.

The car is driving away. We just dropped my stuff off at the house, avoiding Viggo's demanding kisses, and we're going to shop for a Halloween costume.

"No Catwoman." That was the only instruction.

I'm dressed again in some of Maggie's clothes. I can't complain; the dress she gave me is gorgeous, but a bit too virginal for my taste. The skirt flows around my ankles, and the top is a beautiful scoop neckline, showing off my tits a tad too much. Or at least that's what I thought when I saw Viggo eying my cleavage, with a ballet of aubergine veins moving straight down

to his pants. Considering the kiss he gave me before I headed back to the car, I'm guessing he liked it.

Are we a thing now? Just because we came on each other?
I have no idea how respectful relationships work. I have
nobody to talk to about this. Maggie is here, but I'm certain
that whatever I say to her, she will report to her brother.

The car stops, and we get out on a busy street.

"Do you know anything about a book?" Maggie asks out
of nowhere, interrupting my thoughts as I glance around
the various shops.

"A book? What?" I ask, surprised. I mean, I know a book.
I know many books. There are many books out there, aren't
there?

"A wolf book." The gorgeous brunette is now looking at
me. She bends her head to the side—the cat twin thing.

I stay silent, waiting for more.

She advances toward the first shop on our list. "Some
kind of old book the werewolves might be looking for. It
has my brother worried."

Fear rushes through my body. I know the book. The old,
smelly thing is better left alone. I don't speak, and that may
be a mistake.

Maggie turns to face me, her eyes flashing with a new light
of curiosity. "You do know something, don't you?"

I take a deep breath. "The book is best left alone. The
wolves were taking it too seriously, so I stole it... and destroyed it."

Maggie's eyes widen, which is quite a funny sight to witness. "You did? So, they had it?" She pouts. "I hate when my brother is right."

"Right about what?"

"That's the reason your ex-pack made you an Omega. Starting regrouping and all that shitty stuff they do. They are just following this stupid Bible of werewolves."

I pinch my lips, not wanting to say more but satisfied that she is calling it the same way I am. Yes, she's right, and that's the exact reason I stole the damn thing.

Except I didn't destroy it. It's hidden, and well hidden. In a place no one knows but me.

"Why is it so important?" I ask. "It's just a book."

Maggie waves a hand. "As long as it's destroyed, it doesn't matter anymore. There was a lot of information in it. We just need to make sure that no overzealous alpha ever reads it."

I catch up with her, my heart booming in my chest. "Well, technically speaking, they all read it, I think. At least they tried. One of them was translating it... I think that's what he was spending his days doing."

"Right... of course... they don't speak the old language."

"If this language is as old as the freaking smell on this damn book, yes, they don't speak it."

Maggie laughs, and after a few seconds of intense staring, she returns to shopping mode. I'm glad for the change of topic. The book is safe. They can't find it. Whatever is left will never be translated.

This will be fine.

The shop we are in now is one of those temporary Halloween pop-up shops that only exist for the season. The night has fallen on the city, and it's giving the whole shop a scary ambiance. It's spread over three stories, each dedicated to a specific area of Halloween. I am looking at the plan in front of me with a dubious look. I don't want to be a Catwoman, sure, but then what do I want to be?

Superheroes, clowns, princesses...

Those are not very scary, but then I'm not sure I should be scary. I pout and follow Maggie, who seems quite decided on which side she's going, unbothered by all the looks we are receiving on our way. To be fair, a beautiful, six-foot-tall, pale, red-eyed woman would obviously attract some attention.

We cross shelves filled with masks, capes, fake vampire teeth—Maggie glares at those—until we reach the women's section.

Maggie chuckles, and I eagerly wait to see what she found.

"Really?" I scoff, looking at the fluffy white wolf's ears she's holding.

"There's a tail that goes with it."

I catch the headpiece, trying not to notice how similar it is to my actual wolf ears. As a joke, I put it on my head. "I'm pretty sure your brother has high hopes of me dressing sexier than a wolf."

I see Maggie frowns, and I know she's thinking about it.

Oh no.

"Well, I guess it depends on what exactly your plan is with my brother?"

Double-oh-no.

I take a deep breath and put the fluffy ears back on the shelves, almost with regret. I miss my wolf.

"We are not lov—"

"Lovers? Yeah, no offense, girl, but your screams earlier kind of made you lose credibility on this topic." She winks, grabbing random objects from the shelves.

I place a strand of my hair behind my ear, blushing. "It's just…"

She glances at me, excited, as if finally an answer to the biggest question in her life was coming. "Yes?" she pushes, her eyes wide open.

"I have been hurt before, not that long ago…"

"The Kyle guy."

"Yes, the Kyle guy. It's hard to… open myself… but your brother, he's so different from what I thought he would be."

"Yeah, he's good with women, my brother." She smirks. "I've got to be honest, I'm not sure why he's so into you."

"Ouch!" I throw a pink magic wand at her face in retaliation.

"You know what I mean. You're beautiful, obviously, but it's like he met you, and he was into you."

I stay silent for a minute. "Isn't it what happened to you and Gregory?"

"He told you this story? Well, Gregory was half naked on a battlefield, covered by the blood of his enemies, singing the war songs of his clan. That was hot. I'm not judging. As far as I am concerned, I'd rather you protest a bit and fight him instead of all those women just throwing themselves at him for his money or status."

"Well, he offered to pay for my flat…"

"He has never done that to anyone before. Let me give you some advice—"

"No!" I interrupt, my hand in front of her face. Under her hurt look, I feel obligated to explain. "Last time another woman gave me 'advice,' she told me to open my legs and play nice before they all come to me for their fun."

Maggie straightens, tense, staring hard.

I don't stop. Tears bubble in my eyes. "And then one of them was going to rape me if not for your brother attacking our home. So, no offense, but if you were gonna tell me to open my legs and be his personal slut to get nice things in exchange, the answer is no. That's not why… that's not why… I let him touch me."

Maggie steps cautiously toward me. "That's not what I was going to say." She rolls her eyes at my sniff and gives me a little tap on the shoulder, saying, "There, there."

I laugh uncontrollably.

She frowns, crossing her arms. "I'm sorry. I don't know how to react to you people always crying." She shakes her shoulders and catches me by the waist, bringing me to her side and advancing down another alley. "You should have told us what happened at the pack. It's exactly what we want to stop. What I was going to say is this: my brother won't take what you don't offer. When he's gonna take, he's gonna give back." She stops and looks at me, a playful expression on her face. "If I were you, I would take what he's willing to give. Just don't break his heart, or I'll break your arms."

She catches a weird white outfit and puts it in my arms. "Go try this on. Little Wolf." She smirks. "Let's drive my dear brother to the edge of his sanity."

CHAPTER 20

MINA

Viggo's house—my house?—one of the oldest buildings in New Orleans, has become the lair of a wild Halloween party. I haven't seen him since yesterday, as it seems he was out on some punishment business king stuff. I missed him.

I am standing at the balustrade, letting my eyes navigate over the crowd below me. Dancing, sweating. The few who are wearing white are fluorescent under the neon light, their teeth bright. Pretty sure I can spot some fangs already. Actual fangs.

"I may as well go and have fun," I mutter. I finish my drink, some weird wine mixed with raspberry, in a gulp. I grimace as the strong liquid hits my throat. As I climb down the stairs, I pull on the bottom of my dress, trying in a desperate move to make it longer.

Yesterday, after various struggles, fights, and death threats, Maggie convinced me to indeed come as a wolf. A little wolf. I sigh when I look down at my outfit. It's definitely on the sexy edge and far away from what I usually wear.

I have those fluffy white ears she found at the shop stuck on my head, and I have done two French braids to keep my hair in place—because I do intend on dancing. Maggie pulled me to the hairdresser's and convinced me to go back to my natural hair color. Despite my loud protests, I'm glad she did. My outfit? Gosh. I managed to convince her to let me wear my usual boots. She groaned because they were not white, but I won the fight. I didn't win the other fight, though.

Now, here I am, wearing a sparkly, short, tight white dress with hems covered in fake white fur, as well as satin white gloves that end in fur. I'm also wearing some sexy-as-heck thigh-high stockings that stop right at the edge of my dress. Let's not mention my belt, ending in a pretty, fluffy white tail on my back.

When I left the bedroom, blushing, I was ready to burn Maggie. Now, as I finally arrive down the stairs, I understand that I am far from being the sexiest woman in attendance. Still, I'm glad Viggo didn't see me with all the lights on. He's not here yet, even though it's supposed to be his party. I'm unsure how he's going to react to this costume. Hopefully he will like it. I would not mind getting more of him tonight.

Maybe tonight's the night?

I shake my head. This is a bad idea. Sleeping with a man whom you are technically still kind of lying to? Nope. That's just plain bad.

A tug on my hand snaps me from my naughty thoughts, drifting dangerously toward a naked Viggo.

I turn to see Maggie grinning at me, her eyes and teeth simply terrifying under the neon lights. "Come and dance, little wolf!" she screams amid the loud music.

I giggle and follow her on the dancefloor, which is the stoned paved area of their house, now decorated with many Halloween-specific decorations. After this stressful week, I'm ready to have some fun on my night off.

My new 'flatmates' don't joke about parties. For some reason, I suspect the decoration has more to do with Maggie than with Viggo. Fake cobwebs are spread all around the court, some of them hanging low with some black shapes in them—I'm guessing fake spiders. I sure hope those are fake. A DJ is vibing in his corner, wearing what seems to be a Godzilla costume. The crowd is a funny mix of obvious tourists—probably going to get eaten tonight—and even more obvious vampires, barely containing their fangs.

Maggie pulls me toward an empty pocket of space in the middle of the yard, and we begin to move. I let the music take over my body, and our bodies sway with the rhythm; we are screaming, laughing, singing songs we probably don't really know. I haven't really partied in a long time. A long, long time.

My body knows what to do, and my hips follow the pop beat of the music.

Maggie smirks and moves closer to me, eyeing something above my shoulder. She starts a languorous dance against me. The wine I had earlier must have cancelled any kind of inhibition I had because I'm more than happy to play her new game; better her than any of those guys around us. Our hips are so close we are dancing as one, in rhythm, my hands on her shoulders while she holds my waist firmly.

She giggles. The sight of Maggie giggling is... terrifying.

"What?" I yell, trying to cover the sound of the deafening music.

"My brother doesn't seem to like our show."

"Your bro... what?" I turn. That's who she was looking at.

The king stands there, in a suit—must be disguised as a banker or something—his red eyes fixated on us, on me. His lips are in a thin line while another guy talks to him, but Viggo seems to ignore him.

I pout and turn back to Maggie. "You're getting me in trouble!"

"Oh girl, this is nothing! Do you want to get into more trouble?" she asks, a smirk on her gorgeous face.

I laugh and nod, then I rotate on my heels, placing my back against her front.

"Clever girl," she says.

We start our dance again, my ass swaying against her hips, and her hand grabs mine to guide me. I lock my eyes with

Viggo, who is still standing there, not missing an ounce of the show. That's when other men get closer to us. I can see the snap in his face, his fangs out. In one second, he is on us, throwing an exasperated look at his sister. Maggie laughs behind me, and I try holding back my smile.

"The king is joining us! Hail the King!" I say, then let go of Maggie's hand to catch his tie, bringing him closer to me.

"You're searching for trouble, Little Wolf," Viggo whispers to me, his lips brushing my cheek.

Before I can answer, I realize Maggie has left, so smoothly that I didn't even feel her leaving my side.

I chuckle and nuzzle my face against his chest, placing my arms around him. I am a tad tipsy indeed. As if there was a sign, the music slows down, and we can start moving together on a calmer rhythm. I take a deep breath, inhaling his scent of musk and pine.

"Did you have fun with Maggie?" Viggo asks.

I look at him, catching his red eyes, which are stuck on my cleavage.

"Sorry that I was not here today. Had some vampire rebels to deal with in Atlanta. Could not make it back before the sun."

I nuzzle closer. "It's okay. Yes, we had fun, even though I'm never letting her pick my Halloween costume ever again."

He smiles and pulls on my tail. "I kind of like this," he whispers, brushing his lips on my red-painted ones.

"Don't pull on my tail." I whine. "From where I'm from, it's considered very rude."

I love how he laughs. Finally, someone who gets my sense of humor. That he's a thousand years old should have me worried about said humor.

He bends over me, catching my chin in his fingers, his eyes too serious. "I'm sorry for what you went through with your pack. You should have told me. I would have happily killed them."

I stop breathing. Of course, Maggie would have mentioned my meltdown to him.

I escape his hold to bring my face back against his chest. "It doesn't matter now. When you attacked the pack, you actually saved me without knowing it."

"I should have known," he whispers. "When I saw your state, I assumed maybe you were consenting. You were so... still bratty, still strong, still trying to defend the ways of your pack. Marco should have died on the spot. Those bruises. I'm sorry, Mina."

He holds my face so tenderly one would never think he could break me with one snap of his fingers and kisses me, claiming me, in front of his entire court. Army? Whatever the vampires around us are. I don't care. I'm too busy taking it all in, ready for him.

He stops the kiss to my disappointment, and his face seems darker. He even bites his lips. Such a mortal thing to do. "We need to talk about the book you stole from the wolves."

I tense in his arms.

"And about how you destroyed it."

I push him away. "Like I said to Maggie, the book is better left alone," I snap and start heading toward the door leading to the stairs. My perfect happiness is gone in an instant. He has a way of ruining the mood.

I climb the stairs, and he calls my name. Before I have time to turn and throw a vase at him, or maybe even my fluffy ears, it starts. The screams. I freeze and look at Viggo. He obviously heard them.

He snarls. "Get in my room, close the door, now!"

I don't protest. Whatever it is outside, there won't be much I can do. It's not the full moon, so it can't be werewolves. Whoever thinks that attacking the King's HQ is the idea of the year might not be the brightest person.

I scramble into his room and lock the door. Not that a simple door would do anything against some weird monsters, but I'm ready to run in any other shape. Maybe shift as something small? Like a mouse? What if they find me and eat me? That would be a gruesome death.

"Don't know what you're thinking about, but please, don't stop. I could watch this tight ass all day."

I gasp and rotate, searching for the growly voice that just spoke. A smell reaches me, strong, musky. A wolf. Outside of a full moon. Walking toward me. On all fours. Talking.

Okaaaay, that's new.

Besides the fact that it's not a full moon tonight, when werewolves are in their animal shapes, they don't talk. They can communicate if their bond to their Alpha is strong enough, but it's barely some words here and there. Nothing close to a full, perverted sentence.

"I'm not sure you know whose bedroom this is," I say, glancing around to see if he's alone. He's a big, grey wolf with a black stripe on his back. I don't think I have met him before.

"We do. It's okay. I won't hurt you." The wolf sits down on his butt, giving me the innocent look of a puppy who just peed on the couch.

I roll my eyes. "What do you want, then?"

"I am with your pack—"

"Not my pack anymore. I left. And if it's about my debt, tell Kyle that I have plenty of money to pay him." Well, Viggo does, and I'm pretty sure he won't refuse me. Maybe I could even convince him to snap one neck or two while he's at it.

"It's not about the debt. They're ready to forget about the debt, about you running, about you stealing."

I scoff. "Are they now?"

"I can see that you were still working on seducing the king," the grey wolf says.

"This is really not your concern. I am *not* part of the pack. And any request they gave, I didn't follow."

The wolf lets out a growl. I know this sound. It's disgust. Wolves are very judgmental.

"So, you're dancing like a whore with him because you want this? They were right about you, I guess."

"If you have nothing nice to say, I can scream and call the king. Let's see what smartass stuff you can insult me with then."

The wolf makes a weird sound, a mix of a scoff and a laugh. "They told me you were stubborn. We want you to stop seducing him. This is too risky; you can't... fuck him."

I straighten myself, done with this bullshit.

He interrupts me. "Did he tell you he went back for you? To the pack? Asking expressly for the virgin white wolf?"

I tense. Viggo had no way of knowing my wolf was white. Maggie went straight for the white ears earlier, didn't she? How did I miss that? Still, it doesn't mean anything.

"So what?" I retort.

"Do you think he's with you because he... likes you?" The wolf makes a strange scoffing sound again. Asshole. I liked it better when werewolves could not communicate. "He knew you were different. He knew the pack needed you for what's coming, and he wanted to keep you for himself instead."

"What the heck are you talking about?" I mutter, my fists clenched.

"The prophecy they told you about. We need you. Leo made a copy of the book before you stole it. He translated it. We need a virgin white wolf. Turns out they're quite rare to come by. Kyle was a fool to let you go."

I shake my head. "Even if the king knew that detail, he doesn't have any use for me; he would have been better off killing me."

"Are you dumb, Mina? Kyle told me you were not the brightest. This spell? It's not only for werewolves. It can work for vampires, too. And I can promise you, you'll be better off with werewolves."

My mouth is open, but no sound can come out of it. Is this true? It could be true. The waves of betrayal crash over me. Saving the world from crazy werewolves? My ass!

The door opens wide, barely holding on its hinges, and I am not sure if I am relieved or furious to see Maggie stepping in. Her angel costume is covered in blood.

She growls and jumps onto the wolf, not worried about what a bite could potentially do to her. I don't wait a single second more. I run out of the room, leaving Maggie to her slaughter. I need space and time.

I run down the stairs, barely glancing at the slaughter still happening outside. I head straight to the basement. Maggie showed me earlier that old secret passages were leading to one of the streets outside. I open the heavy wooden door and jump into the dark corridor, away from the carnage. My heart is broken.

CHAPTER 21

MINA

I RUN THROUGH THE corridor, disoriented. This place used to be the secret route for alcohol smuggling. Now it's just a terrifying, pitch-black, start of a horror movie tunnel, and I am the dumb teenager running straight into a trap.

I can't see a damn thing. I stumble and fall into a wall, hissing as my face meets the cold stone. Spiderwebs brush against my skin, getting stuck to my hair. I let out a sob. Those are not fake.

I should've known. He showed too much interest in someone like me. Of course, something was off. Whatever the prophecy is, it doesn't sound good enough for me to stay and find out. I can smell the virgin sacrifice coming miles away.

Besides my survival, there's unfortunately only one other thought running through my mind, and that's my worry about the king. What if he gets bitten by one of the werewolves up there?

I instantly hate myself. I don't want to worry about him, especially after what I learned. I need some time to clear my thoughts, but first I need to get out. I stop my erratic running and take a deep breath.

Maybe I could shift into a spider and hide here, letting him think I ran away. This is New Orleans. There's no way I can hide in my woman form from an army of vampires and werewolves. Who knows who is winning the fight upstairs? A spider could at least get me out of the house, and then I will pick a better animal to hide as for a few days.

A creak interrupts the silence and my thoughts.

I jump, glancing behind me, but of course I can't see a thing. I know this creak; it's the door I came through.

It squeaks, followed by footsteps echoing along the corridors. I gasp and bolt again, crying out when my elbow smashes into a sharp corner. I wish Viggo were smart enough to put some lights in this tunnel of death. I take a deep breath and place my hands on the wall, following it the same way one would in a glass maze. I walk as fast as I can with my new technique, satisfied not to hit any new corners.

That's when I hear him.

"Mina?" Viggo's voice resonates behind me, making it sound like three of them are here.

I continue walking. This place is a maze, and I sure hope he'll take a wrong turn. I stop to take off my boots and make myself as light as I can, tiptoeing.

"Mina?" His voice sounds closer. Does his voice sound closer? "You do know that I'm a millennial hunter, right?"

Is it a laugh I hear? I bite my lips, not wanting to make the task easy for him, and I continue walking in silence. That's when I see a door, surrounded by a square of lights behind it. That's my exit. I hurry toward it, holding my breath. Instead of a door, I bump into a grumpy ass, hard, bloody, vampire king.

I gasp and hit his chest with my fists, as if those could do much.

He barely reacts, accepting the blows and not moving an inch. "Are you done?" he asks, his voice cold.

"No!" This time, I slap him, hurting my hand, but this is a minor detail compared to the rage and despair I feel.

He catches my arms and blocks them behind my back, bringing my body closer to his. "You need to hear the full story, Mina."

"I need you to let me go, if you really care for me—the way you *said*!—you will let me go. I can survive on my own." I fight back, but there's no point. His hold on me is like iron.

"I will tell you everything, I swear."

I scoff. "Right! Because you people are a model of virtue and truth." I try to kick him in his immortal balls, but of course, I don't reach him.

"That's it." He picks me up and throws me over his shoulder despite my loud protests. "You were curious about the hook in my room? Let's show you what it is used for."

I grumble a strangled noise, punching his back with all my might, but it's useless. I don't give up until we finally reach his bedroom floor. Blood is spilled everywhere, heads without their bodies, furry legs covered with blood. This was a massacre.

"Where was she?" I hear a feminine voice.

I turn my head and see Maggie's long legs, also splashed with blood. I throw some insults at her, but Viggo slaps my ass, shocking me into silence.

"In the tunnels," he says, "running away."

Maggie laughs, then grows serious. "I heard what the wolf said to you. You can't decide like this based on one random guy coming from a pack who hates you."

"Shut up!" I yell, and Viggo slaps me again. I whine, but my body throbs, including my clit. *Great.*

He brings me to the room while I hear Maggie laughing again, then he closes the door and walks decisively toward the damn hook I'm about to learn about. He drops me carefully onto my feet, and in a blur, he has taken off his fancy tie, now covered in blood, and is playing with it, making me gasp at the view.

"Do not even thin—" I start, but instantly I feel the softness of the fabric around my wrists, and the king lifts me by the arms, blocking the tie on the hook. Right. That's what it's for. Perverted vampire stuff.

I don't say a word as I hold back my tears while I barely stand straight on my tiptoes.

"Tell me, Mina..." Viggo whispers, his hand circling my cheek, wiping a tear that has escaped. "Are you ready to listen, or do I need to teach you a lesson first?"

I don't answer and close my eyes, fully crying. "You're like them. You're exactly like them. You know what I went through, and you still play with me."

"I don't... open your eyes."

I obey and look at him; his pupils are fully dilated, and his eyes are cold. He's angry; I can see it.

"Here's the truth. I met you. I knew you were a virgin thanks to your smell. I didn't know you were a white wolf. When I came back home and went through my other copies of the Bible of Werewolves, I remembered the passage about the virgin white wolf. I had no way of knowing for sure, so we went back there, asking for you. I knew they hadn't translated it yet, and I could not smell the book anywhere in the house. We looked for you around, but there was no finding you. We checked every pack for the past six months, looking for you. But nobody had ever heard about a white wolf. So, I thought you were safe somewhere, that you knew what was coming for you, and were smart enough to hide. I had quite the surprise when I saw you again, in my city. Careless."

I'm still barely standing, listening to him, wanting to believe him. "You should have said something. You made me believe you cared for me—" The last words break in my throat.

His face relaxes, his eyes softening as he looks at me. "I do… Little Wolf… I really do." He cups my cheeks.

"The wolf said vampires wanted to use me, too." There's an accusation in my tone.

"Yes, but he lied. This book is only for wolves, not for vampires. I have many things I want to use you for, Mina. None of them involves what's in this book."

"What's the prophecy about? What is this book about? If I'm the one getting sacrificed, I should at least know," I grumble.

"I'll let you read the full translation, I promise. I want *nothing* to do with it. I want to do what you should have done: to burn it and make sure no werewolves ever read it again. There's nothing vampires can pull from it, you're right, but what can werewolves pull? It would endanger us… like during our youth. It would endanger you."

I finally look at him, surprised.

"The book contains a dangerous spell that could help wipe out vampires and make Kyle—or another, I guess—the Alpha of all Alphas." He pauses, as if hesitating. "The spell we know of… the one they probably took some time to translate… it needs a virgin white wolf."

I am shocked. Shocked that he is confirming those damn Alphas are not crazy. That definitely explains the sudden interest in my hymen, even though six months ago, they all wanted to fuck me.

"Is this why you didn't...?" I start to say, self-conscious.

"Didn't do what?"

"Didn't make love to me," I mumble quickly.

He dares to laugh while I'm still holding onto the soft fabric circling my wrists, all traces of his anger gone.

"I can assure you, the only reason you're still a virgin is because I didn't think you were ready for me." He kisses me, and it is exactly what I need. A passionate, perfect, soft kiss. I manage to laugh a bit and nuzzle him. My fear and anger are gone, as if I am under a spell. A love spell. Damn it.

"What does the spell do exactly?" I ask. "But first, can you take me down? I won't run, I swear."

He laughs. "I'm not done with you in this spot, Mina." His lips become a thin line. "The spell Kyle wants to perform needs your purity. It needs a white wolf, which is extremely rare. Werewolves are never white, as they are no longer pure. After the spell, to make the future Alpha of Alphas stronger... hmm..."

"And what?"

"Every potential alpha of the pack would need to take you. The more Alphas, the stronger the pack becomes, strong enough to kill vampires. Strong enough not to depend on the full moon ever again. They would take over the magical world. What you went through with them? It would become the new normal for any pretty woman unlucky enough not to be marked by a man."

Okay, that's not good.

"Well, I don't want to do that!" I exclaim, almost rotating on myself when losing my balance. He seriously needs to take me down.

Viggo laughs and catches me in his arms. "I'm not planning on anyone other than me to try this sweet pussy of yours, my Little Wolf." A frown reaches his face. "The fact that they probably used forbidden magic to be able to shift tonight is the sign that we are too late anyway. Your Alphas are gone; their minds are lost."

"Is it how they could shift tonight?"

"Yes, a powerful spell, not that hard to do for a skilled witch, but so deep in darkness it can take away some of your humanity left. We only witnessed it once, centuries ago—"

"Can you let me down?" I ask again, interrupting him before he gets into a history lesson.

Viggo's answer is a wry smile, and I know letting me go is not part of his plan.

A soft moan escapes my mouth when he starts to undress himself, taking off his black shirt. With a deliberate, slow move, he opens his fly, pulling his pants down until he is out of them. He stands naked and hard in front of me. I lose my balance again, rotating on my tiptoe, but trying to keep looking at him and his gorgeous cock that he is stroking.

"What are you gonna do?" I whisper, alternating my attention between his dick and his eyes, trying to judge how dangerous the situation could become.

"Don't fear, my Mina. I won't do anything that you would not enjoy." He advances toward me and, with one of his hands, rotates me so my back is against his chest, making me shiver at the touch. He moves both his hands on my body, starting on my thighs, slowly, excruciatingly. His cold skin sends me waves of shivers that I am unable to hold off. He moves them higher, following the curves of my hips, my waist, reaching around my breast.

It doesn't take long for him to rip off my dress, destroying it in half despite my shrieks, and grab both my tits, squeezing me.

I can't stop the moan that escapes me as his fingers graze my peaks. My head falls back, seeking the solidity of his chest as comfort. His chest rumbles against me as his hand brushes over my shoulder, as light as a feather. I freeze.

Then his lips press against my Omega marking, soft.

"They marked you...the fools... my poor Mina." His voice is filled with a contained rage, a raw, primal rage, and I wish I could see his face.

He kisses the mark again, his icy lips sending the most delicious shiver through my body. A low snarl rumbles from his chest as he moves his hands further down until he reaches my panties, his fingers curling there for what seems too long. In a second, my underwear has flown away. I whimper as his hand cups my pussy, giving it a slight push. When his finger starts teasing my slit, I'm just losing it.

I moan and start moving back and forth, trying to catch more of his fingers with my body. As an answer, he only growls.

"See," he says, "I knew you would enjoy the hook." He inserts two fingers at once without more foreplay, immediately playing me with skill, his movements rough and fast while his other hand tortures one of my breasts.

My whines grow in volume, and I spread my legs, trying to give him better access despite barely balancing on my feet.

"That's it, Mina. Come for me again. I want everyone in this house to hear you scream."

His raspy voice reaches me from someplace I have already gone.

"Some wolves have survived. I want them to know how well I'm gonna fuck you soon. I want them to know how much of a good girl you really are when a true man takes care of you. I want you to come on my hand, and then I will go to them. Let them smell your pleasure all over me, knowing this will be the last delicious smell they get before I rip their heart out."

I whimper, and in a few seconds, I know the familiar wave is coming, taking over. I lose my balance this time and fall down while I scream my pleasure, his fingers thrusting inside of me with no pity.

I'm trying to catch my breath, barely keeping my eyes open when he moves around me. His eyes are covered in black, and

I can see his cock still hard, throbbing. Viggo catches my chin between his fingers, softly, then brings his hands to my lips.

"Taste yourself," he says, harsh and demanding.

I moan and obey, opening my mouth to give him access. I can taste my juice all over his fingers while he looks at me, fascinated. I give him a wry smile, and I move my lips up and down his fingers, mimicking a blowjob.

He chuckles and takes his fingers away from me, moving further. For a moment, I fear he's not going to get me down from here, but he catches me and moves me up to get me off the hook. My hurt arms can barely move, and he catches me carefully. I raise my head while he unties the fabric holding me. He then grabs me by the neck and pulls me toward his hungry mouth. I whine under the touch of his lips, and I immediately throw my arms around his neck, satisfied.

Safe.

CHAPTER 22

MINA

I YAWN, STRETCHING OUT. It's getting late now, but I want Viggo to be by my side when I fall asleep. It's a miracle I'm still awake after the crazy start of the night.

It's now three in the morning, and my entire body and brain are begging for some sleep. Viggo went and made sure everyone was safe, kicking out the last partygoers, who were dancing in the guts spread on the floor, celebrating their victory.

It's not as if I could have slept anyway, hearing the noise of agonizing wolves for the past two hours, the ones who were unlucky enough to be caught alive.

I know my flatmates are probably torturing them, but I don't care, not with what I learned was in their damn Bible of Werewolves. I told Viggo where I had left the book and promised to go retrieve it with him. He didn't want me to come, talking about safety and stuff, but I didn't leave him a choice. I should have burned the damn thing instead of hiding it.

Road trip! Road trip! Road trip!

Instead of sleeping, which would be the smart thing to do, my brain has been burning, thinking about what I know, what the king knows, and what we can guess about Kyle's plan. The more I think about it, the more I'm convinced that only the Alphas of my previous pack must know about this whole 'let's gang rape the virgin white wolf' thing. I can't imagine any other members of our pack approving this.

Alisha? She's a bitch, with a capital B, but she would probably not tolerate Kyle touching me. Gloria never liked me, but why would she accept this? Not to mention all the ancients and the families we have at the pack. I can't imagine that any mother with a daughter would ever allow a communal rape to happen. I know I wouldn't.

But then you're not really a werewolf; what do you know? My little voice continues nagging me.

As I'm not a werewolf, is there not a risk that their damn spell does not even work? Dumb. Maybe if the Alphas are not around, I can talk the others through it... convince them of what is going to happen and of how bad the whole idea is. We will be there tomorrow, which gives us two days to come back to New Orleans away from angry werewolves on a full moon. Viggo seems to think they would not be crazy enough to pull a forbidden spell again, but honestly? Nothing would surprise me anymore.

I don't have time to reflect more on this plan when, finally, my king returns.

I mean, *the* king. Not *my* king. *Whatever.*

I let out a quiet sigh of relief, and he offers me a smile in return, going around the bed to bend over me, pressing a light kiss on my forehead. His lips are cold, and he reeks of dried blood.

What am I? A child?

I grunt and grab him by his neck, pulling him down and crushing his mouth to mine. I take a deep breath, nibbling at his lower lip while I try to catch his tongue.

"Mina." He groans; his voice is like a deep growl. One of his hands clutches the sheet beside my head.

I pull back from him, lying down on the mattress, ready to go to bed.

"Night night!" I say and start turning away from him, but immediately, I'm grabbed back in his embrace, and I feel his heavy body on mine, molding against my curves. Before I can speak, his mouth is back on mine, hungry.

Passionate.

Intense.

Hot.

Kiss.

I rest my arms on his shoulders, opening my mouth, giving him access, enticing more rumbling growls from the depths of his torso.

I am wearing a long shirt tonight with panties, and I'm blessing my choice of clothes when one of his hands heads up along my leg, the caress so subtle I could almost forget about it, but I can't. His touch is soft but cold, his frozen skin against my burning one. If he were to head higher, he could feel how hot I am for him.

He stops kissing me, giving me an army of wet kisses along my chin, my neck. I tense at his slight nip on my neck. He tries to reach my collarbone, but my shirt seems to derange him.

"It is indeed annoying me, Mina..." He groans.

I chuckle. Of course, he is listening to my thoughts.

He sits on his knees, between my legs, and observes the end of my shirt. His lips thin, and one of his fingers lifts the fabric, tickling me on the way. "These panties of yours are in the way, too." He lifts my shirt. "Hmm."

"What?" I ask. I'm wearing one of my prettiest pink lace panties; it's covering my cheeks comfortably, but the fabric is see-through, and I thought that was quite cute.

"That's really cute." He confirms, following the contour of it, his fingers brushing so lightly it makes me shudder, intensifying my burn.

I moan.

"Mina..." He chuckles, continuing his caress. "You are so wet that I can guess the shape of your cunt through this fabric."

My gosh, I love his dirty talk. I never found it enticing with Kyle. His way of doing dirty talk was all about insulting me and forcing his cock into my mouth.

But Viggo? His words make me even more excited, and I spread my legs, giving him a full view of my body. I lift my shirt slowly, all the way above my breasts, arching my back. He tenses when the shirt is close to going over my tits, and his finger dance gets stronger, now stroking my center, brushing my drenched slit through the light fabric.

I caress my breasts, holding one in each hand, under his fascinated gaze. I grab them both, fist them, squeeze them the way I like it, then I start playing with my hardened nipples. Viggo closes his eyes and throws his head back, as if he is taking a deep breath—even though he doesn't need to breathe—then returns to me, his attention fixed on my hands, his hands caressing me, still through the fabric.

I let out a squeak when he touches my nub through the protection. My breathing reaches a new pace while I continue to torture my nipples, pinching them with force while pulling them. Viggo lets out a feral groan at the view. He reaches for his pants, opening his fly and giving me a view of his gorgeous dick.

I give him a worried look, and he smiles back at me. "Don't worry, you're too tired for tonight. I'm keeping our first time for another night."

Well, I am indeed exhausted but also quite turned on. I don't have time to reflect on how patient this guy actually is. His cock pushes against the fabric, his tip against my wet panties. I let another moan out, spreading my legs a bit more while caressing myself.

With a swift move, he has slid my panties down my legs, dropping kisses along my skin, and I find myself naked beneath his gaze. He changes position, coming closer to my face. My eyes widen

"Are you happy taking me in your mouth, Mina?" he asks, his voice low and deep, stroking himself, his tip already leaking pre-cum.

Images of my previous blowjobs rush to my mind: uneasy ones, forceful ones. I hate that those are coming back to haunt me. So, I nod shyly, blushing, and I wait.

Viggo pulls me to my bottom, sitting on the bed. He rotates me, making me face his legs. I immediately know where this is going, so I place my legs on both sides of him, moving my bottom toward his face. He has the biggest smile, and this makes me laugh, helping me to relax a bit. I'd rather be above him this way. Hopefully, I will have some kind of control over the depth I take him in.

I jump when his tongue starts his amazing ballet on my slit, and I moan under the pleasure, whimpering. He licks my nub, playing with it, nibbling at it, and it's almost sending me straight to climax already. It's time to give back.

I lick my lips at the view of the cock waiting for me and the hard, purple veins that never stop their dance. His tip is huge and wet with pleasure. I can't wait to taste him, to make him mine. I point my tongue out, licking the tip in little circles. He trembles under me. It's hard to focus when I'm so close to climax, but I continue, licking the entire length of his shaft, gently grabbing his balls, playing with them. I hold his cock with both hands and finally take his length into my mouth.

His mouth leaves my cunt for one second, and he groans, grabbing a handful of my ass, squeezing it. Thankfully, he gets back to work. You can say what you want about him, but he's a giver. I grind my pussy over his face, accelerating my rhythm with my hand and mouth. His cum leaks out. When he bites my nub, I have no control over myself. I straighten up, stopping all blowjobs, and I scream my pleasure, mixed with some pain. I speed up my grinding over him, begging for more.

"Again... again, please!" I continue dancing on his face, hoping for another climax to come. Thankfully, the king is generous; long live the King.

Viggo groans something about "insatiable Little Wolf." He moves from under my body, then with a push, he brings me down on my elbows and spreads my legs, giving him full access to my cunt and my ass on display. He presses my lower back, causing me to curve my spine. I moan when his fingers penetrate me. One, then two, immediately starting their violent moves. I know I am not going to take long before climaxing again.

"Come on me, Mina," Viggo murmurs, never stopping his finger fucking.

I am so out of this world that I barely feel when something strokes my butthole. Instead, I squirm harder, waiting for my climax. I whimper when what I think is his thumb enters my tight entrance, but nothing shocks me anymore. The double finger fuck brings me to the brink of pleasure.

The orgasm comes in a wave, growing bigger by the second. It's in a silent scream that I finally come, barely holding on to my knees, scrambling on the bed. My juice coats him again, but there's no shame anymore.

His entire body vibrates, and he rises from the bed in a swift motion, standing at the edge. He brings me toward him, wrapping my hair around his iron fist, bringing my face toward his crotch, stroking himself.

Without hesitation, I adjust myself, still on my knees. I look at him, my mouth wide open, waiting for his cum to fill me, impatient to taste him. His own climax does not take long, and I take it all, swallowing as much as I can.

Viggo bends over me and brings me to his face, kissing me, tasting himself on my lips. "Now Mina... you go to sleep before I lose my mind. We have a long drive tomorrow."

CHAPTER 23

MINA

I STRETCH MY LEGS, holding back a yawn. We did indeed take a road trip. After a much-needed sleep, we left New Orleans around four in the afternoon. The sun was still out, but Viggo took one of those potions the witches prepared for him. I'm curious to know what's in there, considering the face he pulled while drinking it.

The drive to my previous pack is quite long, and we should reach it by midnight. We go through the traffic of Atlanta. The city is still alive despite the late hours, and we drive toward the national forest where my ex-pack lives.

The plan is to sleep there, somewhere, probably in the village close to the pack and the forest, but far enough not to be spotted. I am not happy about strolling right into werewolf territory two days before a full moon with only Viggo.

That we also have to play around the sun is stressful for me, but Viggo seems more than relaxed about it. I'm not the one who is going to become a pretty little dust mound tomorrow morning once the potion's effects have passed, but I'm still worried about it. I asked why he didn't bring a stock of potions with him, and it turns out this specific drink can't be kept once ready for longer than an hour. I would say that witches probably don't want it to last too long, and they are not making an effort to help their vampire friends.

Viggo seems completely unbothered. When I asked him, he chuckled and kissed my hand, and my hand has been stuck in his for the last hour. I don't want to let go of it. I enjoy this light touch, so natural, so innocent, but protective at the same time. We talked a lot during the trip, but we also enjoyed the silence while listening to his eclectic music collection. A silence that was nowhere near being awkward.

Unfortunately, silence makes my brain go wild. I can't stop my mind from twirling around, thinking about what we are.

Are we a thing? Like a couple? Oh my God, are we exclusive? Do vampires do exclusive? Of course they do. What if I am just a toy? Great, another heartbreak incoming. What if he played me? I hate being played.

I spot a green sign outside, finally showing the next exit to my previous town, and I sigh with relief. I'm done with the travel, but mostly I am done with my hectic thoughts.

Viggo glances at me, a smirk on his pretty lips. "Are you tired of my company already, my Mina?" he asks, squeezing my hand. "Or are you done questioning our relationship?"

I narrow my eyes, then look at our linked hands. Of course. How can I keep forgetting about the whole reading your mind thing when we touch?

"It's impolite to listen to others' thoughts, you know that?" I pull his hand toward me, bringing it to my lips for a kiss.

He gives me a burning look. "I can't exactly help it. Your mind is fascinating. So confused, so little self-confidence."

Ouch.

I immediately pull my hand away. This is unnecessary for me to hear. I cross my arms, trying not to let anger take over.

"Mina?" He reaches for my hand again.

I shake my head.

"I didn't mean to hurt you with my words. But you have to recognize that you *do* have some difficulties accepting what's happening between us."

"Well, you know, maybe that's because you kind of lied to me?" I snap, giving him a dark look.

"I sure did."

"Are we a thing?"

He frowns.

I'm quick to continue speaking, mixing my words, confusing myself, and sounding ridiculous. "It's okay if we're not. I mean, no, it's not okay. Am I a joke to you? What am I? I can't go through this again."

I wince and stop talking when he parks the car on the side of the road, not caring about the angry honking from the one behind us. I freeze, crumbling under his heavy gaze, as he turns his body toward me.

"I'm sorry I hurt your feelings," he says. "You went through hell before, and this is your trauma speaking. I care for you; I always did. The day we met, I should have grabbed you, taken you away from them, followed my instincts. I didn't, because I was trying to be a fair king."

He holds my face, and I push my cheek against the cold of his palm.

"Are you really worrying about this? About us?" he asks. "Do you still need reassurance that I'm serious about you and our relationship?"

"I... I... just have been used before... and I don't want to do it again. We have already been so intimate..."

He chuckles, brushing his thumb along my cheek, then locking his eyes on me. "I can promise you, I was not planning on sharing you with any man ever again, nor playing with you like a 'pet,' as you love to call it. I care for you. I'm not a player. Women always know what they're getting with me. You need to accept this if what we have here is going to work."

I take a deep breath, catching his hand in mine and placing my nose against it, enjoying his musky scent.

He continues. "I haven't cared for a woman the way I feel for you in centuries. It's new for me too, but I think I finally found you, and I'm not planning to let you go. Once all of this is dealt with, I was planning to talk with you, about us, about our future."

"You were?"

He chuckles. "I learned a long time ago that communication is key with women. Unfortunately, I'm not the best at multitasking. I need to deal with the wolf problem first."

I laugh.

He brings my lips to his and kisses me soft and sweet at first, deepening with heat until I'm melting into him, offering him passage in my mouth. When he pulls back, he whispers against my lips while I let out a groan.

"Also, if what you're scared of is me playing you, I do not fear promising more. I'm not some little boy scared of commitment."

I give him an interrogative look. Whatever he meant, it doesn't make sense right now.

He smiles and says, "I'm more than happy to offer you a life beside me and, a wedding, before we become more intimate. If that's what it takes, I'll gladly wait. Once we are done with the wolves, we can wait a few months and see where this is taking us."

Okay, now we're talking about a wedding. *Wait, what?*

"That's..." I start, trying to find my words. "Are you serious? But... you're king of vampires. I'm not a vampire."

He grins. "It doesn't matter, au contraire. Besides our love, this could also be a strategic alliance, bringing another species into the crown. It will mean more people will trust us until we convince every magical creature that I can be their leader, too."

"So, you do want to take over the magical world?" I scoff, holding back a smirk. "The werewolf was right, I guess."

This time, he barks out laughing, amusement showing in his crimson eyes. "Yes. I learned a long time ago that magical creatures need some structures, unfortunately. Look at what's happening with the wolves. As soon as a pack hears about their Bible, they're all running around, making poor decisions, hurting innocents. The magical world needs a ruler. Someone strong but fair."

"That's a good point," I mutter.

He smiles at me and gives me another light kiss, even though I would not mind something a bit lower, and then gets ready to drive again.

"As with anything else, there's no pressure on my side. I'm immortal; I can wait. If I had waited for you 1,000 years, I can wait a few more years before finally diving my cock inside your tight and welcoming pussy."

My brain stops working, and I swear I forget how to breathe. I have no time to answer that, he has started the car again after those good words of his. My body can't accept this. In two seconds, wetness takes over my panties. I bite my lips, knowing we can't stop again if we want to arrive and find a place to sleep safely away from the sun.

Damn this guy.

CHAPTER 24

MINA

THE MOON GLOWS IN all of her glory above the falls, revealing luscious trees and moss. The full moon is in two nights, and I can't help thinking that we need to be out of here before those woods are filled with grumpy wolves. I'm still not sure that coming here with no sort of reinforcement was the smartest plan, but my road trip companion does not seem worried.

I take a deep breath. This feels like home, though. I do love New Orleans and my newfound freedom there, but I love the forest more. I close my eyes when Viggo's arms surround my waist. He sneaks his chin between my neck and shoulder, embracing my body against his.

Perfect.

Cuddles in the best place ever? Done. If we were not here for 'business,' it would be even better, but I have a promise to hold. I rotate, making sure to stay in his embrace and catch his eyes. His look is soft, not appearing even slightly tired after our long drive. He readjusts his position against me, lowering his head to rest it against mine, the simple gesture he always does, sending shivers through my body.

"What was your plan for sleeping?" I ask.

"There's a town twenty minutes from here. We can find a motel, I'm sure. Hopefully, with dark curtains." He chuckles.

I pout, looking at the forceful water above us, so noisy I can barely hear him. "How about I show you my secret spot?" I murmur. "That's where I hid the book."

Viggo gives me an interrogative look. "You hid a book at a waterfall? Maybe it's destroyed indeed, and I needlessly worried."

"Nah." I laugh, and I grab his hand, guiding him. "Trust the process."

I direct him to the entrance of my special spot, my hidden cave, right behind the flowing water. I watch my steps carefully as I go in; I have learned that the floor is quite slippery. My heartbeat races. I hope they didn't find this spot and the damn book.

After a few more meters, it's like a new world welcomes us. A world of soft glow, water sounds, and mossy walls. I smile when I see a few objects I left here: a blanket, a pillow—both stolen from the pack; they can add it to my debt—and a notebook with some of my drawings. Lastly, the famous book. I kneel by a small cavity and place my hand in it, immediately feeling the book under my fingers. I grimace. I know I am touching dead skin. Viggo has confirmed that the cover would probably be some dead animals or maybe even a human—hence the smell.

I pull it out of its hiding place and give it to Viggo, my fingers shaking. His face relaxes, and he takes it delicately, his lips in a thin smile.

"Thank you, Mina. This will be hidden in our vault, among the few other specimens we have of it." He looks around the cave, curiosity showing on his features. "No sun here in the morning?"

"No, you're safe."

"Perfect." He catches me by the waist, pulling me in for a kiss. "May I share your one pillow and blanket?"

I chuckle when his hands rub my back, and I nod, heading to the small comfort we can have tonight. I'm planning to use him as a pillow anyway.

We are lying down peacefully, as planned, my head resting on his chest. I gladly gave him my pillow in exchange. His skin is frozen, probably made worse by the humid atmosphere, so

I'm the one using the thin blanket. We have been in the same position for a while in a peaceful silence, listening to the water sound around us.

I glance at him. His eyes are closed, and there's a smile on his lips.

"Why are you smiling?" I ask.

"The noise. It reminds me of my home." He opens his eyes, looking at me. "I will take you to Norway one day, to the shores where our village used to stand, deep in a forest, still barely untouched. Too wild for the modern world to step into. We have the most gorgeous falls and fjords there."

"Another road trip? Sign me up." I chuckle and nuzzle back my head against his chest, silent, empty of any heartbeat.

"Maybe for our wedding…" he murmurs.

I immediately get back up and look at him. So, he is being serious.

After a few seconds of my silence, he adds, "I'm kidding. We don't have to get married. This was just an offer to accept or decline. We can take our time. I have never proposed before. This used to be quite easy thousands of years ago. Now it seems there are many rules for men to follow."

I don't give him more time to fall into his explanations. I jump on him, riding him while my lips head straight for his. We kiss, and my heart flutters.

"Let's talk about it when we are clear from this incoming psychopath wolves thing going on… okay…" I kiss him one more time.

He grabs me under my butt, clenching it. Viggo moves me back against his chest, lying by his side.

I sigh with contentment. "So, they're not gonna be able to do the spell, right?"

"Well... nothing can be certain. We don't know how much exactly they have translated, or if they found another book. They need the watch—safe at home—the virgin white wolf—to my dismay, still a virgin." He laughs when I hit him on the arm. "And the full moon." He looks at me with a snarky smile on his lips. "They only have the full moon for now. I'm not planning to let them catch you."

I bite my lips, looking at him from below my eyelashes. "We could maybe get rid of the virgin part?" I give him a soft kiss on the part of his chest accessible to my mouth.

Viggo laughs. "I was joking. I do have a sense of humor, you know. I have been practicing."

"Well, I'm not joking." I look at him, his eyes crimson, the snowflake pupil showing. I smile and move my body closer to his, getting him to turn toward me. I need him against me, above me, inside me.

Viggo kisses me without hesitation, taking my lips as if I am his last dinner, his hand rubbing my back softly but getting harder, demanding. It's not long before his touch reaches the curves of my ass, grabbing me again. He moves me onto my back, lying on top of me. A growl reverberates deep in his chest as he intensifies the kiss, never letting go of my lips, while one of his hands heads toward the edge of my dress, brushing me. He's going to realize how wet I'm already for him.

He growls, and I know that's it. He knows how much I want him.

"Are you sure, Mina?" he whispers. "Now that you offered it, I don't think I will be able to stop once I get you naked and squirming under me... hearing all those nasty thoughts of yours. I'm strong, but not that strong."

As an answer, I move my hands down to be able to remove my panties, enjoying the salacious look he watches me with. He helps me to pull it along my legs, leaving traces of wet kisses on my skin. He removes his shirt, and I take in the sight of him. I'm already squirming with desire at the view of his muscular chest and the V-shape heading straight down his pants. Pants that need to be taken off, right now.

We are finally naked against each other, heat against cold. I let out a moan when his thumb rubs my clit, helping itself to my juice, driving me already way too close to the edge. His finger slides in my drenched core, slowly, while he keeps his lips on mine, moving in harmony. My rapid breathing is *not* in harmony anymore as I am overwhelmed with pleasure, enjoying his touch.

Viggo finally inserts one more finger into my pussy, making me whine with content. I spread my legs a tad more to give him better access.

"That's it, my Little Wolf, open wide for me... show me that tight pussy of yours." He groans when I spread wider, pushing myself against his fingers. The back-and-forth is already driving me close to insanity. I'm so wet I can barely feel him anymore.

"More... I need more," I murmur, taking his hand in mine and leading his movement.

"Whatever my lady asks, she shall receive."

I squirm when the stretch comes, letting out a groan, my breath rapid. Viggo uses his fingers to fuck me for what seems way too short, and I know he is intentionally keeping off my clit, holding my climax back. I can't stop looking at him: his gorgeous body and those purple veins heading straight to his impressive cock. I swallow at the thought of finally having this inside me, all fears gone, replaced by my growing impatience.

He takes away his hand, and I sigh, rubbing my nipple. Viggo strokes his dick with a deliberate slowness. His tip is covered in pre-cum, calling for my lips to claim it as mine, and I'm ready to beg him.

"Please..."

"Please, what? My Mina?" he whispers, a wry smile showing on his lips, his fists accelerating around his length.

"Just take me... please..."

He hisses—yes, *hisses*—and moves between my legs, one hand close to my head to hold himself while he pushes against my drenched entrance. I gasp and let out an unhinged moan, rubbing my nipples harder, pinching both of them, pulling them. My senses are already overwhelmed with the sensation of him entering me.

"That's it, my Mina. Pleasure yourself while I take you, while I make you mine." He pushes harder, stretching me.

I wince at the pain from his large cock, moving one of my hands to circle my clit.

"Good girl. I knew you were a good girl as soon as I laid my eyes on you... so eager to please a man who takes care of you... and I will take care of you, my Mina."

I yelp, rubbing faster while he gives one stronger push. This is it. I'm finally getting fucked. My screams grow louder when he gets deeper inside me, growling at the sounds escaping my mouth. I place my hand against his chest, stopping him, taking a deep breath in.

"Do you want me to stop, Mina?" he murmurs, dropping a few kisses on my face.

I shake my head. There's no way in hell he's stopping now. I keep my hand on his chest and bite my lips. His eyes remain on me as he grabs both my hands, moving them above my head. He kisses me, begging for passage into my mouth, nibbling on my lips, sucking my tongue. My body opens to him more until he moves again inside of me. The sharp pain takes over my senses, and I'm in a twirl of pleasure mixed with it, moaning from the slow thrusts he's doing.

He growls, never stopping the kiss. His hands hold my wrists in an iron grip while he continues his back and forth. Slow, careful, but passionate. He didn't lie before. He's truly making love to me. This is not fucking.

"Let me touch you." I beg him, and thankfully, he releases my hands, moving onto his knees while pulling my body against him, both my legs held by his hands. I extend my hands, grabbing his forearms, and hold on tight to them while I thrust my core against him, taking him deeper.

"*Mina*!" he growls, his eyes only showing pupils.

I giggle. "Take me harder, My King." I thrust again, yelping at the feel of his cock buried deep up into my pussy.

He doesn't say another word, and his grip tightens on my hips, and I know I'm in for a ride when he starts fucking me. His powerful thrusts go as deep as my body allows. The pain is gone, and I am a mess of sweat and screams, letting him have his way with me. Tears escape from the pressure building in my core until I finally feel my favorite wave taking over my body, making me explode, stars blocking my view.

I am still moaning when he slides out of me and moves his fingers inside my throbbing pussy. I know what he wants, and I'm more than happy to oblige. It does not take long until my second orgasm reaches me, and I squirt all over his hands and legs while he lets out another hiss.

I laugh at this noise, moving a hand to hide my smile.

"What are you laughing at, my Mina?" he asks, a light of curiosity in his eye. He stands up, towering over me, stroking his cock.

"You hiss!" I answer, barely able to talk.

He laughs. "Well, I'm a vampire, after all." He gives me a dark look, accelerating his self-pleasure. "How about you use this mouth for something else now?"

I move onto my knees, closer to him. Bending my head back, I give him my sluttiest look, opening my mouth wide and holding his thighs against my palms.

"That's it, keep that mouth of yours open. That's my good girl... taste me. If you miss one drop, I'll take you so hard you won't be able to walk tomorrow."

I shiver and close my eyes when the first drop of salty liquid reaches my tongue. I swallow whatever reaches my mouth but make sure to miss some bits. When I reopen my eyes, he's still standing over me, trembling.

Then he looks at my mouth. "You missed some."

"Oops?"

CHAPTER 25

MINA

THE RUSHING WATER PULLS me from my slumber. The constant roar, echoing through the walls of our cave, finally gets to me. I let out a wide yawn, keeping my eyes closed and savoring the sensation. My body aches in new ways, all delicious and satisfying. Viggo is still spooning me, his chest pressed into my back, his arm falling heavily over my waist. I smile. This is the same way we fell asleep after he made love to me. And fucked me. A few times.

It's morning time now—well, probably afternoon—and I need to use the bathroom. Back to reality.

I shift carefully, trying to slide out from under Viggo's possessive hold, trying not to wake him up. My gaze flicks at his face. Not even a twitch.

Right, I forgot. Tiny-Red had mentioned something about old vampires like the twins being almost impossible to wake if they hadn't had their full seven hours. It would be funny if I were not stuck under his arm.

Suppressing a sigh, I lift his limb with difficulty, resting it back with care on the blanket. Viggo still hasn't stirred. Perfect. Time to head outside.

Once free, I step outside the cave, paying attention not to get caught by the water's flow, and inhale deeply, enjoying the natural surroundings. The sun is still high in the sky, but I'm guessing it might be around two or three in the afternoon. We slept longer than I expected. I stretch my body while also letting out another yawn, enjoying the few droplets of water reaching my skin thanks to the wind.

I take care of nature's call, then I decide to enjoy the silence a bit, leaving Viggo to sleep. I wash myself quickly, enjoying the cold water on my sore body. Although I don't especially want to get rid of Viggo's smell on me, I'm too sticky to stay this way all day. I sit on my favorite rock by the water's edge, dipping my feet in the cool water.

After a few minutes of bliss, I look at the cave behind the falls, starting to feel impatient. I love being here, but this reminds me that my ex-pack is barely ten minutes away. Sunset is not for at least another four or five hours.

We have the book. We should go. Every minute we spend here is asking for trouble.

I lean back, my hands planted in the ground behind me, tilting my face toward the sky. I should have brought my phone instead of playing Robinson Crusoe, trying to guess the time according to the angle of the sun. It's fine, I'll—

The wind shifts.

Something is wrong.

Too late.

They come out of nowhere.

They jump on me in a blur of bodies—the Alphas. My blood turns to ice. I don't get a chance to scream or fight back against the one who grabs my arms. He wrenches my arms behind my back, while others stop my throat from screaming. That's when a new smell reaches my nose. Strong, but sweet. Chloroform. I thrash for the very few seconds I have left, but I know it's useless. My body betrays me, growing heavy, limp. My vision gets blurry, and the roar of the waterfalls fades.

And then, darkness.

I wake up groggy, a searing pain pounding behind my eyes. My wrists are tied in front of me, rope biting into my skin. I try to clear the fog caused by the drug. I blink and look around, holding back a sob. That's when I see her, with her freaking perfect, bouncy curls. Alisha.

She's sitting on a chair a few feet in front of me, cautiously, as if the chair were not good enough for her Luna butt. Her arms are crossed tightly under her chest, and she is wearing her usual pout, the one she does when things don't go her way. "Did you really need to come back, Mina?"

I roll my eyes while eyeing the way my wrists are tied. "Trust me, I didn't want to."

My heart is thudding in my chest. Did they find the book? I sure hope they didn't. I also hope they didn't find Viggo, sleeping like a stone in the cave. How much of his surroundings can he hear when he sleeps? My heartbeat races at the thought he might be hurt or dead. Well, dead-er. I can't handle losing him, not now.

"Where's the book?" Alisha whispers, rising from the chair.

I bite my lips. If they don't have the book, they don't have my king.

I sit up better, trying my best to get comfortable on the cold stone floor, my heart pounding. "I don't have the book. You have to stop them, Alisha. If you knew what they're planning to do…" I shake my head, thinking back to what the king described to me, holding back tears.

She stays silent, her eyebrows raised. That's when it hits me.

"You knew?" I whisper.

"Of course I knew," she snaps. "I have a PhD in ancient Nordic culture, remember? I guessed a while ago you might be the one they needed, and I didn't want to take a chance. I tried to help you, Mina. Not that you were very thankful. Why do you think I told you to get fucked as soon as possible? I even convinced Marco to fuck you." She gets closer and murmurs, "They had no idea they needed you for the spell. Leon was taking ages to translate what I had finished weeks prior."

I freeze, rage taking over. "You sent Marco to rape me?"

"No. I sent Marco to fuck you so that we would be rid of this silly spell they want to do. It's not my fault if you were not smart enough to let him have his way."

I have a few things to answer to this, but she interrupts me. "When I told you to pick the strongest male, I didn't mean a freakin' vampire."

I scoff. "Yeah, right, great advice you gave me." I'm not sure how much she knows about my relationship with Viggo, but I don't plan to elaborate.

She ignores me. "Now we're stuck. Because of you. The Alphas want to complete the damn prophecy. Alpha of Alphas. Do you have *any* idea what that means?"

"Yes!" I blurt, trying to get rid of the ropes around my wrists. "That's why you need to help me stop them. Let me talk to the others in the pack—"

She laughs bitterly. "No, girl. You don't get it. What's bad is that my man is going to fuck you for this spell. He's still obsessed with you. He thinks he's going to be the first to get in your pants. Typical."

I stare at her, stunned. "Seriously? You want to stop the spell just because you're being a jealous bitch?"

She leans closer, her voice a hiss. "You literally *just* needed to open your freaking legs, Mina. And now..." Alisha stops her motivational speech; her head snaps toward the stairs, her expression shifting. She steps away from me quickly, putting distance between us.

My stomach twists. Heavy steps on the wooden stairs going down to the basement. They're coming.

I glance at the tiny window, but there's still daylight out there.

"What time is it?" I whisper, as the Alphas step into view, blocking the window, each one more menacing than the last.

And none of them look happy to see me.

CHAPTER 26

MINA

THE FIVE ALPHAS ARE looking at me. Marco, Leon, James, Chad, and Kyle. Yes, there's a Chad. They look unimpressed, giving me the same look they always used to give me, as if I am the lowest of the low—and also, a pain in their necks. I thought Viggo said that Alphas came and went while I was away, but from what I can see, they're the same assholes who were already there before. They probably played around, knowing vampires were spying on them.

Kyle glances at Alisha, who glares, not backing down.

"You can leave, Alisha," he says.

She scoffs and heads to the door under the glare of Kyle and some laughs from the others. Alisha pouts at me before she leaves, as if all of this is my fault.

"Mina. Thanks for coming back," he says once his girl-friend has left the room.

"Go fuck yourse—" I start, but the wincing pain of a fist in my cheek interrupts me, and I yelp under the strength of it. Marco. Of course.

"Watch your language. I thought a few months away would have taught you manners," Marco says, cracking his knuckles.

Freaking asshole. I tighten my jaw. Blood is already pooling in my mouth, and I spit it out.

Kyle steps forward. "As I was saying, Mina. No more games. You talk, or you fucking suffer, until we finally get this spell done."

A chuckle escapes my lips. They still have no idea that Viggo is nearby. As soon as he wakes up, he'll know where I am. I'm ready to bet those guys are not going to live long. I hope they're not going to live long. Hopefully, Viggo will forget about being a 'fair king' for five minutes.

Kyle looks confused but does not speak.

Marco does. "You seem quite confident for a little bitch who's going to get her asshole fucked until we know what we want."

My heartbeat rises.

Kyle tsks at him. "There will be enough of that tomorrow. This is not going to make her talk, trust me." He looks at me. "Some people in the pack are not big fans of our idea already; no need to add more sex."

I roll my eyes. "Maybe I feel confident because you don't have the book, you don't have the watch, and if you think I can't handle your tiny dicks, then you're wrong."

Also, I have a grumpy vampire king coming for me as soon as the sun sets. I glance at the window. I think it's getting darker, but it could be my eyes deceiving me.

"Do you still have the book?" Leon, the translator, interrupts.

"Of course not. I burned it. What do you think I am, stupid?" I sure hope my poker face is better than it used to be.

Leon sighs. "Such a waste." He places his glasses better on his nose. "Thankfully, I made a copy. I would have preferred to keep the original one, though. It would have been more impactful when we try to convince other packs to join us."

Other packs?

"There are already five packs together. Kyle, you can't have more than that. This is insane!" I address him, trying to search for whatever kindness could be left in him, but there's nothing.

Viggo was right. First the Omegas, then the madness.

"It won't matter to you anymore. This is necessary. Vampires are taking over. Even you should know that. Look at what's happening in New Orleans. Do you want to be a walking bag of blood for the rest of your life? They have slaughtered hundreds of wolves over the centuries."

Yes, I kind of know that already because I had the other side's version. I decide to stay silent on the topic. "*Nothing* is happening in New Orleans; everything is under control.

Vampires, witches, mortals... they all live in peace. It's actually really well organized."

Kyle scoffs.

I continue. "We can all live in peace if we want to. It's working there in the city; there's no reason why it would not work everywhere."

"Where's the watch?" Leon interrupts my talk of global peace. He's sitting on the chair previously occupied by Alisha, crossing one of his legs above the other.

I smirk. "Surrounded by an army of vampires stronger and smarter than you."

"If we have to wait for the next full moon, we will. We just need the watch and the book, and we will let you go after the spell. You don't need to die. If you want to go back to New Orleans to be the vampires' favorite little pet, you can. The day will probably come when we meet again." I love how Leon tries to be the good cop in all of this, as if I would believe him.

I almost scoff when Marco's eyebrows shoot up. He clearly doesn't agree with the idea of me leaving.

"Great, thanks." Now is not the moment to tell them I'm not a virgin anymore.

They turn their heads when the door upstairs opens.

I hold my breath, hoping to see my favorite face in the world. I quickly disenchant when I spot pretty black high heels. Definitely not the king. Instead comes a purple head I know too well.

"Maddison?" I am stunned. My freaking colleague. I knew she didn't like me.

"Hey."

"What do you mean, 'Hey'? What the fuck are you doing here?" I scream.

She advances toward Marco, using the feminine gait she always shows when male customers are at the bar. He grabs her waist, smirking at me. She places something in her hand, and my heart is ready to explode. The watch. It has to be. A round, golden, vintage-looking watch.

"Thanks, babe," Marco says, grabbing the watch. He gives it a disdainful look and throws it to Leon, who winces and glares at Marco while he carefully wipes it with his sleeves.

Marco glances at me. "Mads and I have a history. I was quite surprised when she told me about her new colleague."

That explains how they found me, I guess.

"How the hell did you steal this from the king's house?" I ask.

"Halloween." She shrugs. "While others were making a mess, I sneaked in. I'm a witch. It was easy to open the vault. I'm done with vampires dictating their laws in New Orleans. It's not as idyllic as you seem to believe."

If I could throw stones at her, I would. Kyle steps in front of me, cutting my view of her and Marco, who is busy grabbing her ass.

"So, Mina… I don't believe you. Where's the damn book? Don't make us hurt you. We don't need you to be pretty for tomorrow. We just need your pussy, and we need the book."

Leon flinches.

"I thought you made a copy?" My voice is a tad too smug for the situation.

Kyle sighs, rubbing his eyes. "Yeah, yeah, but we need the book for the spell. The watch needs to be placed inside it. Where. Is. It?"

Leon sighs. "Great job. She's never going to tell us now."

Kyle catches my jaw between his fingers, squeezing so hard it brings tears to my eyes. "Oh, trust me. She will."

The first blow comes without warning. I expect to be hurt; I don't expect it to happen so fast.

Kyle's fist cracks across my cheek, snapping my head sideways. Pain explodes in my jaw, and blood rushes into my mouth, the metallic taste taking over my senses. I fall sideways, landing hard on my shoulder and screaming.

Before I can breathe, a boot slams into my stomach. Air whooshes out of me, and I gag, my breathing interrupted. I curl into myself, instinctively trying to protect my core with my tied wrists.

"Get up," Kyle growls.

"Fuck you!" I whimper.

I just have to hold on a while longer. They can't kill me; they need me. I need Viggo to wake up and hunt me down.

I'm trying to breathe still, trying to see through the haze of pain and tears. Another kick drives into my ribs, followed by another. Three of the Alphas are hurting me, not keeping any of their blows at bay. Kyle, Marco, and Chad are enjoying themselves a tad too much for my taste.

My body jerks with each impact, and when one reaches my cunt, the pain soars through my body. I cough and spit blood onto the floor, bringing my knees up high.

Marco grabs my hair, yanking my head up. He forces me onto my knees, despite the pain in my ribs, begging me to stop moving. "Still awake, Omega?"

I glare at him through the tears. Blood drips from my nose and runs onto my lips. He smiles, then, in a strong movement, he slams my head against the stone wall with a dull *thud*. The world spins. I'd rather pass out.

I am dripping blood all over, my entire body screaming. My hands and knees press into the floor. I see their feet moving around; I hear them laughing aloud. I am still hoping someone from the pack will intervene, but it seems clear nobody will now.

Another blow hits my stomach, leaving me crunched in a ball again. Then my thigh. Then another punch, straight to my head, landing on my ear and causing a new world of pain. Pain is everywhere now—throbbing, burning, screaming under my skin.

They take turns.

Like it's a game.

James pulls me up on my feet and holds me, his arm under my breast, but I can barely stand. Why am I still conscious? I want to sleep.

Marco kicks and reaches my knee. The crack is deafening, and the pain is so intense that this time I let out a scream, a wail of despair.

"Finally." He laughs, "I like it better when they scream."

A boot crushes down on my ankle, grinding the bone. I choke on a cry, a broken sob escaping my lips, in so much pain that no screams can come out of me again, only a silent one.

Marco moves his hand on my neck and squeezes, cutting off my air. I claw at him, but it's pointless.

Kyle gets closer. He has found a wrench. He lets the metal of the tool follow the curve of my jaw before asking me.

"Where's the book, Mina?" He follows my jaw, my collar-bone, my breast, then brings the tool to my cunt, pressing it. "As I said, we just need your pussy tomorrow. We can go all night. Nobody cares about you, Mina."

I lift my head an inch. "Go to hell." I sob.

At the light of fury in his eyes, I swallow and wait for the pain.

CHAPTER 27

MINA

IT'S THE SCREAMS THAT wake me up from my painful dreams. Where am I?

I wince as I struggle to open my eyes. I can only see a shred of red on one side, and I sob, terrified that they've taken my sight. I don't heal like werewolves. I can heal, but the process is closer to any other mortal than a werewolf.

What happened?

I remember trying to hold on, clenching my jaws so hard it hurt, but not wanting to give them the satisfaction of my screams and pain. I knew the night would come soon. Night meant shadows, and shadows meant him. I just had to survive until Viggo arrives. *They didn't find him; he's okay.*

I wince as I make a wrong movement, my ribs aching with every breath, and I know for sure something is broken. Many things.

Assholes.

I let out a strangled cry when I take a look at the bloody mess on my knees.

Memories flash back. It's the pain under my waist that refreshes my blurred mind. The sob that comes out of my mouth is strangled, raspy. It's a silent scream that comes out when I remember the wrench used to destroy my skin, my bones, including in my pubic area. I was held by James, fully offered for Kyle to hit me relentlessly on my lower parts. The pain is indescribable. Is it broken?

My body gave up. I passed out. Did my mind give up as well? Did I betray Viggo? I can't remember.

I fight to push myself up onto my butt, dragging my weight to reach the wall to lie against it. My legs can't move from under me, and my hips barely accept the movement. I let out a cry. My fingers are numb, but I still flinch when they brush against something sticky—blood. My blood.

The screams outside grow louder. Desperate. Men yelling. A woman shrieking. Then a crack—gunshot? No, werewolves don't do guns. Something else. My vision is so blurry I can't make out the time. I can see only darkness. Red.

How long have I been down here?

The door opens wide, and I gasp, squeezing myself against the wall. I need to protect what's left of my body. My pulse races as footsteps approach, heavy and fast. I can only see a shadow through the blurry crimson, and I whimper, waiting for the next shock.

Cold. Something cold touches my face, brushing it. My king.

I wail, flinching as I lean into his touch.

"Viggo." My voice cracks, more a whisper than anything else. The salt of my tears drips into the open wounds across my face, sending yet another kind of pain.

"Shh, my Little Wolf," he murmurs, "I've got you now."

His growl echoes in the small room, and he tears the chains from the wall. Viggo gathers me into his arms with a gentleness that makes me cry harder. He mutters something under his breath, and despite the care he uses to lift me, my body screams in agony. I hang in his arms like a broken doll.

I don't even have the strength to wrap my arms around him. I want to. I want to hold on and never let him go, but I can't. I am so weak; my limbs are cold. Another whimper escapes my mouth as he carries me up the stairs.

"Viggo!"

I recognize the voice. Maggie. I can't see her. My vision is so foggy, filled with tears and blood. I hear her moving closer, her heels clicking on what seems to be a wooden floor. Only Maggie could come to war while wearing her Louboutins.

Then silence. A silence that says too much.

"I can't," Viggo whispers.

"She's too far gone," Maggie replies softly. "Look at her. The closest hospital is an hour away. She won't survive the drive. You want to keep her? Convert her. *Now*, brother."

Convert me?

To which religion? I don't really like religions, but I don't have time to protest. I just want to sleep, safe in my king's arms.

CHAPTER 28

VIGGO

THOSE MONSTERS.

I see red—blinding, burning red—the same shade I saw when our tribe was destroyed a thousand years ago. The same color that fueled my rage when I woke up as a vampire. My ears ring with a high-pitched sound, and my entire body is screaming at me with a single command.

Revenge.

"All survivors lined up. Outside. Now." I snap at some of my soldiers, bringing their attention to something other than my dying Mina, lying still in my arms.

I kneel in the wet grass and lower her down as gently as I can, waiting for the wince of pain, but there's no reaction. I can hear her heartbeat, but it's way too weak for me to afford to wait.

I bite my wrist, hearing the satisfying sound of my fangs transpiercing my skin. Without further ado, I place my bloody opening against Mina's mouth.

"Drink, my love." I cradle her head in my other hand.

It doesn't please me to convert her this way, with no ceremony, no party, and no consent. I know Maggie is right; we have seen enough mortals dying of various wounds to know that her frail body would not survive the trip to the hospital.

So, vampirism it is. I hope she will forgive me for choosing life instead of death.

She drinks, barely, but she does. Her throat bobs as she swallows. She just needs a few drops to survive, but I am not taking any chances. I insist that she has more, keeping my wrist against her lips. Maggie is sitting on her knees beside Mina, holding her hand with the same tenderness she cares for Gregory.

When I am satisfied with the amount she drank, I press my lips on Mina's forehead, giving her one last kiss. I break her neck in one swift movement.

A few members of the pack gasp.

I whisper, "See you soon."

I lay her body down in the grass for now, holding back my first instinct to run and slash everyone's throats as I take in her state. I stand up, fists clenched, digging into my skin, jaws so tight it makes my head throb.

I let my eyes roam above all of them, assessing the situation. Our army arrived fast and strong the night before the full moon. Those fools didn't stand a chance. I should have listened to Mina's concerns. My army was already marching, and we could have joined them. But I'm not one to regret past decisions.

There are many men in the pack—a disturbing ratio actually—but some women too, and some children. The five Alphas are in a line, forced on their knees by some of my soldiers.

I unclench my fists with difficulty. Blood runs along my fingers, dripping on the grass. My senses are too exacerbated. My feelings also are.

I growl when Maggie steps beside me.

There's a concerned light in her eyes. "No children, Viggo, remember."

I don't look at her, focusing on the shades of crimson blurring my vision, calling for slaughter. "Even if they may come after us?" I ask.

The mothers grab their children, whimpering and placing them behind their backs—as if they could stop me.

I hold the looks of the ones fool enough to be brave.

They always come; we learned that over the centuries. They grow up; they wait, building their hate and vengeance over the years; and then, they strike. I don't mind when they do; it seems only fair. I understand revenge.

Maggie steps closer to me, standing between us. I know she's trying to bring my attention back to her. "I highly doubt that

Mina would ever forgive you for hurting children, or some of the women, especially after what she went through."

I hold back my low growl.

Maggie commands me. "We kill the Alphas; we burn the house. We make a statement. We make them kneel."

I swallow my rage, forcing my attention away from the pack and back to my Mina. She is still lying on the grass, her body inert, but I can already see the benefits of my blood running through her veins. Her legs straighten, and her cuts are closed.

She'll live.

"They were going to let it happen, Maggie. They let them torture her, even though she was one of them. There were enough of them to fight back against five Alphas."

Maggie doesn't flinch. "You know how the wolves act when surrounded by so many alphas; they have no control, they're too scared. When you have a family, you don't want to take the risk of being the one getting hurt. It could be their daughters one day."

"Exactly!" I scream, pointing my hand at them. "It could be their daughters. They still didn't raise a finger."

Maggie steps closer, placing an appeasing hand on my arm. "I don't want you to be this kind of king. Not if you want to rule over all the species one day."

I close my eyes. I fucking hate it when she's right.

"Fine." My voice is cold. "Take the children away. We will keep you tight in the magical barrier for tonight and tomorrow night while you shift. The Alphas will be tortured for the next month. Every day. Every hour. Every possible and imaginable torture that has ever existed. And you, adults, who would have let such a communal rape happen, you will watch. Every day. Every night, until the next full moon. When the month is done, you will be brought safely to your children."

I hear sobs, probably relief ones, and murmurs.

"I have been kind enough. Every year, on the anniversary of my fiancée becoming a vampire, you will be reminded of what happened here. Let it be clear, for every wolf out there, that if something similar happens again, there will be no werewolf left alive in this world. Not on my watch."

I turn away, dropping to my knees to gather Mina into my arms. I leave fast, before being ready to come back on my last words and kill the last of them.

CHAPTER 29

MINA

A HIGH-PITCHED SOUND DRILLS into my ears. My sensitive ears. I moan and bring my hands to them, trying to protect my poor eardrums from the atrocious noise. I refuse to open my eyes. I perfectly remember the sea of red from when I last woke up, and I'm not ready to accept losing my sight yet.

A soft touch reaches my face.

I jump and immediately relax when a metallic, musky, warm smell reaches my nose. *Viggo.*

"Mina?" His masculine voice resonates, almost making me tremble, so deep, so powerful, so... hot.

I take my hands away carefully, leaving my ears in the open. I inhale, taking a deep breath, ready to open my eyes and discover if I'm blind or not.

That's when it hits me.

I was not breathing before.

A whimper escapes from my mouth as I open my eyes, panicked, my hands clenching at my throat.

"Mina! It's okay, you don't need to breathe, you're safe, my love..."

Viggo leans above me, his crimson eyes bright and looking at me with care, his lips in a thin line.

"Viggo?" I mumble, stopping to claw at my skin, and start moving around, then realize that I'm not in pain. Not at all. I am in his bed, back in New Orleans, and I take in everything around me.

Him. His smell. Maggie, not far away, is watching me carefully. Tiny-Red has a hand on her waist, the silk of her dress shimmering under his touch. Dust floats around. A spider moves through the left corner above the bathroom. *Wow.*

I search for Viggo's eyes; he is smiling, both his hands touching my face, palping me as if making sure I'm here. "I had no choice, my Mina. You were gone. This is the only way I could keep you."

I don't need him to tell me more. I know exactly what it means.

I gasp when I realize I'm moving my legs, my entire body, without a wince of pain. I almost want to cry, but tears don't reach my eyes.

I look back up at Viggo. His brows are furrowed, and concern reflects in his expression.

"Are you scared I'm gonna get grumpy at you?" I ask him while observing the way his shirt is following the contours of his strong chest, sculpting every single ab that can possibly exist.

"I would have rather you agree to it, true."

"You saved my life. Why would I be angry?"

Maggie interrupts. "Mortals can have funny reactions to eternity. And about our diet. People are so sensitive."

Gregory nods to his wife's words but I can barely notice anything else because my mind can't seem to focus on a proper conversation. Instead, I am lost again in the contemplation of Viggo's body. His hands, so strong yet so soft when they touch me. The way his lips do this smug smile of his. His legs, held tightly in black pants, muscles showing off under the fabric.

I sigh.

"See anything you like, Little Wolf?" Viggo is smirking, all traces of concern gone.

I roll my eyes and squeeze my legs together. I almost died. I went through hell. Why can I only think about his hands on me and the way his cock could stuff me right now? What kind of weird vampire thing is this?

Maggie chuckles. "I won. Give me the money." She extends her hand toward Viggo.

"Later, Maggie," Viggo mumbles.

"What did she win?" I ask, licking my lips when I spot Viggo's Adam apple.

Purple veins run over it as he swallows. He stands up from the bed, to my immense regret. "When a new vampire is created, they usually go through three stages, not always in the same order."

"Mhm." I am not really listening to him. How can we get rid of Maggie and Gregory so I can get fucked? Ideally, quite hard.

Oh, wait.

I look up. "What... are those three stages exactly?"

Viggo chuckles and glares at Maggie and Gregory, who seem to understand the message as they start heading toward the door.

"I guess we'll see you later," says Maggie.

"Bring some food," Viggo says in a demanding tone. "A pretty one."

I squeeze my thighs harder. Now they're gone, and desire awakens inside of me, burning me. My clit throbs between my legs, begging. The fire intensifies as Viggo removes his shirt, and I whimper at the view of his strong body—and the V, still there doing its sexy V stuff.

I jump on him, my hands fumbling with his fly. I need him. Now.

My king laughs aloud but happily lets me open his pants, only laughing louder when I rip the fabric away, destroying what I'm sure are some of his favorite leather pants. It's okay; he has many of those. Finally, he's naked in front of me, his dick hard and dripping pre-cum, calling for my tongue to taste it, to devour it.

"I need you so badly." I whimper and I move to his cock, not bothering with any foreplay, taking him in my mouth, not paying attention to his grunts.

He catches my head, moving in rhythm to my mouth while I hungrily devour him.

He growls when I give him a small bite. "Angry, hungry, and horny. Three stages, Mina. You're starting with the horny." His fist clenches harder on my hair when I manage to fit him entirely inside my mouth. Looks like becoming a vampire gave me a few new skills.

"Not that I am complaining about it," he mutters, thrusting in my mouth harder, forcing me to take him deeper as I grab his ass and hold him tight.

I raise my eyes to catch his. His pupils are dilated, and I wonder if mine looks so pretty and creepy now. I move along his shaft, taking him deep, enjoying his filthy groans every time his cock hits my throat.

I am ready to jump when a knock interrupts us, but Viggo places an appeasing hand on my shoulder. "It's okay, Mina. Just some food. You're gonna need your strength for our first fuck as vampires."

I am grumpy.

Oh, my God, *so* grumpy.

I need to fuck him. But I also need to eat. I need to kill.

A man is thrown into the room, and the door shuts behind him. I can hear Maggie's muffled laugh. He's handsome, tall, and showing off some modern tattoos. His frightened eyes make me hornier. And hungrier. Fear licks his body. His heartbeat reaches an unnatural speed, his breath unstable. And his smell.

A moan escapes my mouth, and I jump to my feet. I stalk toward him. "He smells so good..."

Viggo follows me, still naked and stroking his cock. I lick my lips at the view, but this smell. The amazing scent of metal and jasmine is keeping my short attention span away from Viggo.

"If you want to, he can pleasure you, my love." Viggo comes behind me, his arms encircling my waist while I observe my prey.

"Pleasure... but... that's cheating."

He looks serious. "This will be the only time I allow you to be touched by another man. You can grab the chance now..."

I walk closer to the victim, listening to the way his heartbeat is accelerating. Fear. Not a hint of desire in there.

"No," I say, and I turn to Viggo, grabbing his dick in my hand, pulling him softly to me as he lets out a hiss. "What I want is for you to take me while I feed on him."

Viggo groans, and in a fast blur, he throws the other man on the bed with no ceremony. Will I be as fast as he is?

In another blur, Viggo pulls chains from a drawer—I didn't know we had those—and our victim is tied up to the bed, begging us. His fear drives his smell to another level of deliciousness, and I lick my lips.

I jump on the bed, landing with elegance and so much grace that I feel proud for one second. Then I sit on the man, my legs on each side of his waist, and lower myself, aiming for the neck.

I moan when Viggo moves behind me, caressing my ass cheeks, and in a few seconds, my dress and my underwear are gone.

"Bite him, my Mina," Viggo says.

It's quite instinctive. My fangs grow in my mouth, and with the tip of my tongue, I brush them too hard, making myself bleed. Enticed by the taste of my blood, I dive my fangs into his skin. My core grows warmer at the squeals he lets out. I have never been a hunter; I have always been prey. Now, I understand the feeling better. Hunting is way better than being hunted.

As I take my first drink in, Viggo brushes his cock along my drenched pussy, playing with me, rubbing it on my clit.

I stop drinking. "Viggo... please..." I squirm under his touch.

"Please what? My love?" and he moves his cock to the entrance, pushing slowly. Too slowly.

"Please fuck me... just... fuck me." I dive back into my drink as Viggo finally slams inside me, resulting in my screams gargling around the warm liquid falling in my throat.

CHAPTER 30

VIGGO

As I slam harder into her, Mina mewls her pleasure, her first orgasm already reaching her. Vampires are lucky. Our senses are so exacerbated, pleasure is easily obtained, especially after our conversion, our fresh blood running high.

I hiss as she screams. "Harder! Harder!" She thrusts her hips against mine while she's still trying to correctly feed on our victim, who has already passed out.

I grab her hips, holding her in place while I come out of her welcoming pussy, laughing when I hear a gurgle of complaints.

"Viggo!" she groans, turning her head to look at me, with this adorable, grumpy frown she always has on her face.

"Yes? My love?" I tease, spitting on my cock and fisting it.

"Get back in there."

"I want to try something new."

She raises an eyebrow. "I hope for you that something new involves your dick inside of me. You don't want me to reach the 'angry' stage now, do you?"

I laugh. I love my vampire Mina even more than I loved my sweet shifter Mina.

"Don't worry about that, my darling. Now, get back to work on this guy, and show me that virgin ass of yours."

There's a flash of desire in her eyes, and this instantly makes me even harder, if it were possible. As she returns to drinking her meal, she pushes her pretty ass up in the air. The arch of her back is probably the sexiest I have ever seen, placing her tight hole in perfect position for me to play with it.

I let out a growl as I bring my mouth to her perky ass, listening to her whimpers as I play with her hole. My tongue gets active and circles it, slowly at first, then forces her tight entrance to welcome me. I bring one of my hands to her cunt, brushing her nub softly, covered in her wetness. Mina lays her head on the man's chest while moaning, her hands clenching his face—poor guy still passed out—gripping him, her eyes closed, her lips covered in blood.

I fuck her with my tongue, spreading her cheeks, enjoying the taste of her while I actively pleasure her with my other hand. Already, her new climax is reaching its peak soon. As her moans get louder and her body starts tensing, I stop my tongue ballet and instead bring my cock to her tight entrance, pushing softly.

"Viggo," she whimpers, opening her eyes, looking at me.

"It's okay, my love; it won't hurt as much as you think it will. You're a vampire; you instantly heal any kind of pain." I push harder, groaning under the tightness. I rub her clit faster, and as I do, Mina starts losing her mind, her hands gripping her victim's head as she rocks back and forth, pushing her body against my length.

I hiss and hold her hips firmly with my hand. "Move this ass of yours on me, Mina. Show me you can take me."

She lets out a depraved moan but obeys, and to my pleasure, she starts lowering her ass along my shaft, tensing under the intrusion as her tightness takes me in, inch by inch. I rub her faster, now wanting her to reach her orgasm as she takes me in.

Her screams get louder with my touch, and she gets to take me deeper, but not there yet. I stop rubbing her.

"No! Don't... stop..." She looks at me over her shoulder.

"Sorry, my love. You don't get to come until this lovely hole of yours can hold my entire cock inside of it."

Mina whimpers and continues her back and forth; I can't look at anything else but her body welcoming me deeper and deeper, as her groans get louder.

"I can't wait anymore... Mina," I whisper, and I grab her hips with my left hand while my right hand goes back to her throbbing clit, circling it with fervor.

Her moans are out of this world as she continues her soft rocking along my dick. I dig into her hips with my fingers and pull her against me, forcing my entire cock inside of her, resulting in a new wave crashing onto her. I feel her orgasm vibrating through her entire body.

I barely pay attention to the sickening crack that resonates under her as I fuck her ass now relentlessly, enjoying our skins hitting each other at each of my thrusts. I'm proud of her as she takes me all the way, panting her pleasure. I'm not long to come and I don't hold back as I fill her ass with my cum, our eyes locking as she glances at me with her naughty smile.

Fuck. I love her.

I enjoy lying down against my Mina, her body still soft but now strong, hiding a phenomenal force. And covered in blood and cum. The poor guy they threw in our room is long gone. The crack I heard earlier was his head, crushed between Mina's hands during her powerful orgasm.

She sighs beside me, like a happy kitten waking up from its nap. Her hand follows the lines of my abs, tickling me. When I glance at her, she's showing this tiny smirk she does when she's planning to do something naughty.

I let out a low chuckle, bringing my body closer to hers. "What are you planning, my Mina?"

She laughs and pushes me against the bed. Baby vampires are always so strong; thankfully, it does not last long. I can easily fight back if I need to, but I am happy being pushed and mounted by her. I take in the delightful view, her perky tits teasing me while she starts moving her hips above me, brushing her pussy covered in our cum against my cock.

"I am not tired," she sings and puts her hands on my chest, holding herself steady while continuing her divine dance, rubbing her clit against my dick, already hardened.

I chuckle. "I bet you're not. How would you feel about visiting the wolf prisoners? I want to make sure you're happy with the way we do things."

She moves one of her hands below, grabbing my throbbing cock, fisting it with dedication.

"Way to cut the mood, Mr. King!" She gently plays with my cock and I thrust into her touch, closing my eyes. "If we go down to see them, I'm afraid I'm going to kill them straight away." She throws a look at the dead body beside us. "And I have just learned there's no fun in that..." she adds with a whiny voice.

Gosh, my vampire Mina is perfectly unhinged, and I'm here for it.

CHAPTER 31

MINA

Viggo manages to convince me to leave the bedroom so his servant can clean the mess we made. A dead body does start smelling bad quite fast, and it's not nice for our sensitive noses. I'm unsure if I should be worried about how little I cared for the man I killed. Did I become a monster?

I struggle to keep a straight face as I watch the servants take the body out. I turn to Viggo. "Why don't I feel bad? I have never hurt anyone before. Shouldn't I be... still a little like the old Mina?"

He smiles and comes to me once he is done putting on some pants. "No, this is perfectly normal. Empathy comes later for vampires; the fact that you are 'worried' about being a monster proves that you are doing great. Most of the new vampires don't bother at all. They just grab what they want."

He seizes me by the hips, caressing my back through the silk of my dress. "Remember, blood is our water. We need it. We can eat other stuff, but without blood? We die. The same way mortals would die in a few days without water. You can't feel bad about something that is natural, something that makes you survive."

"Sooo... no vegetarian vampires, I'm guessing? Like... animal blood and stuff?"

"Vegetarians? What? No! Such a funny idea."

I chuckle and bring him closer to me, dropping a kiss on his chest. He didn't bother to put on a shirt yet. He'd better do this quickly if he wants me to get out of this room.

He gives me a soft kiss on the top of my head, and his hands start heading dangerously down my back to follow the curves of my ass. As he reaches the end of my dress, his veins start their dances again. He must realize I'm not wearing any panties.

I let out a laugh and bolt away from him and his grabby hands, walking back toward the door, licking my lips. Viggo has a hungry look on his face, and I can guess his dick is pushing against the fabric of his pants as he roams my body from head to toe.

"Are you coming?" I ask, still walking back, but I catch the hem of my dress and lift it, teasing him while I show off my bare pussy to him.

"Mina," he growls.

He is ready to pounce on me, but I run this time, trying out my new speed. Along the corridor, down the stairs, straight to the basement. The walls stream in a mix of blurry colors, and I hit myself on a few corners. Fine. *Many* corners. I laugh ecstatically. This extra speed is so fun.

A gust of wind stops beside me. It's Viggo, his pupil's dilated, his jaw clenched. He grabs me by the hair and brings my face to his in a possessive way, forcing my lips to open under his tongue.

I am ready to beg him to fuck me right here when I hear them.

Screams. Desperate.

The fear, the most delicious scent of fear reaches my sensitive nose. I stop our kiss. Locking eyes with Viggo.

"Music to my ears," I whisper, and my heart flutters at the view of his bright smile at those words. I can barely contain my excitement, and after a last kiss, I turn and push the door. "Wow."

I have to be honest, I was not expecting *that*.

As I enter the room, I take in the satisfying scene. The Alphas are lined up and tied on various poles, tables, or hanging from some hook, while my entire pack is packed tight inside the five cells behind them.

I quickly let my eyes inspect the cells.

"Where are the children?" I turn to Viggo, ready to hurt him if he touched the kids.

He sighs. "Safe. With another pack that I trust." He walks, elegant and half-naked, in front of one of the cells. "Only the Alphas are being hurt, my Little Wolf, but their flocks will endure the awful job of being witnesses, power-less. For the full month."

He turns to them, snarling, a rage I have never seen before showing in his usually peaceful expression. Gone are his happy, puppy-like, relaxed features. "They will watch as we bring the ones they chose for leaders to their knees. They will cry as we dismember them piece by piece. At night, their dreams will never be the same, and when they think they have finally forgotten their time here, we will remind them." He rotates to me, advancing like a predator, locking his gaze on me. "Every year, we will celebrate your birth and their downfall."

He catches me by the hips and, with a savage growl, kisses me ferociously, then stops. "They will learn what happens to traitors, to cowards, and more importantly, they will remember."

I hear whimpers and murmurs, but I don't care. I jump on Viggo, surrounding his hips with my legs, begging for the passage in his mouth, hungry. I wiggle as his hands grip my ass, holding me tight while his fingers brush my intimacy, already igniting a fire inside of me.

A throat clearing interrupts us. I groan but turn to look at Gregory—the culprit.

"Don't you want to know what we are doing at least?" Gregory asks, outrage showing on his face while he shows off a paper.

Maggie has the same, and she is wearing square, red glasses. She doesn't need glasses.

"Why are you wearing those?" I ask.

"It's fashionable," she says as if it is obvious. "Not like you would know anything about it. Hopefully, in one century or two, I can convince you to redo your wardrobe."

I snort. "Sure. And what's... this?" I point to the papers they are holding.

I'm intrigued, and I jump away from Viggo, hearing his growl of disapproval as he grabs me back and sticks his body against my back, holding me fiercely.

Gregory's face instantly brightens, and it's with too much excitement that he explains. "Torture Bingo!"

"Tort—what?" I scoff. Vampires are insane.

"Bingo!"

"Gregory has been a big fan of bingo since he learned about it," says Maggie, and she gives a quick glance to her husband, her eyes filled with love.

"Hmm... okay..." Who am I to judge?

"Wait! Wait!" Excited as a child, Gregory takes a step. "See, we each have our list, and every time Josua here"—he nods toward the awfully creepy man who is standing in the cell, so tall and pale he looks like the Slenderman. Simply terrifying—"starts a new torture, we do bingo!"

He glares at his wife. "Maggie thinks she knows everything about ways to torture a man; she always disagrees on the ones I want on my list."

Maggie rolls her eyes. "That's because I always win this game. You have such a wild imagination." She looks at me. "Sometimes, like all things, simpler is better."

Gregory catches his wife, playful, and I have never noticed before, but his eyes show impressive sparkles of orange mixed with the red. "I don't usually hear you complain about my wild imagination."

Maggie giggles and moves her glasses down her nose, watching him over the frame. "If I could blush, I would be blushing right now."

They continue bickering, but my attention is now back on the five Alphas. It's hard to see exactly what they have been through already in barely a day, but I feel satisfied. Or close enough.

"You are missing one. Two, actually."

Viggo frowns. "I thought there were only five of them?"

I walk toward the cell, searching in the shadows for the two faces I'm looking for. I grin when I find them, huddled in a corner, trying to hide behind others.

"Open the door," I say to Josua. "Please." I may be a vampire, but I can still be polite.

As the thin male plays with his keys, I hear Gregory behind me. "Yes! The angry phase is my favorite one!"

"I don't know, I kind of like the horny one too," Maggie says.

Josua opens the metallic door, and I step inside the cage. Viggo is not far from me, tense. I feel strong, powerful, immortal. And definitely a bit angry. As I walk, members of my previous pack spread, leaving a passage for me to go through. Their fear has increased, and I'm glad they finally know the feeling of 'please, not me, pick someone else, anyone else.'

With a fast movement, I grabbed the first woman by her hair. With no hesitation, I throw her across the cage. She lands like a doll right outside it, her screams resonating like the most delicious song in my ears. Then, the second follows the same path.

I step out. "Meet Alisha, Kyle's Luna, a rape matchmaker expert. And Maddison, traitor." I pause, then look at Viggo. "She's a witch, though. Is it bad for business?"

He smiles and gives a simple nod to Josua.

Both women are brought onto two of the available crosses. "I'll deal with the witches. Besides, she's the one who thought she could steal an important watch from my home."

I look at him. "Well, she did."

Viggo gives me the biggest smile. "She stole *a* watch, not *the* watch. We just wanted to know who the traitor among the witches was."

I am speechless. "You knew?"

"Of course, my love, I have been playing this game for a while. I didn't think they would be crazy enough to enter my home and steal from me; they proved me wrong. I had my army already marching to your pack while you and I were...road-tripping."

I smirk. "I did love our road trip."

He joins me and kisses me, his hands grabbing me by the hips, possessively, and I know that if he could, he would fuck me right now.

He steps back. "So, do you want them to die too, my love?"

I let my eyes roam over them while they are being hanged. "Yes, death sounds pretty good. Same as the Alphas, please." I say to Josua, who simply bends his head slightly in agreement.

An amazing idea comes to my mind. "Except for one thing." I look at the five Alphas, in pain, terrified, but still looking at me as if they wanted to kill me. "Cut their dicks off, please. Now." I sit on the available chair, crossing my legs, waiting, while I listen to the screams.

Vampire Mina? Yes, please.

Epilogue

VIGGO

I STAND STRAIGHT AS I witness her walking along the aisle. A beauty out of this world, a smile that has condemned me to an eternal life by her side, her eyes brightening as she takes me in. My Mina.

Her wedding dress must be the most exquisite I have seen, perfect for her, hugging her curves as if my gods crafted it. Her crown is made of fresh flowers, the ones that are still growing over Brigid's tomb, as if our old friend wanted to be part of this. She picked a black dress instead of your usual white wedding attire, and it suits her new 'her' to perfection. Her red hair is left in a mess of curls and the color is contrasting on the dark of her outfit.

I can only notice her, and from the corner of my eye, I see the shadows of her friends moving slowly in rhythm to stand not far from her, showing with pride their crimson dresses. One—Ms. Marble, I believe—adjusts her flowers while another pulls a tissue from her bag. My Mina insisted that her friends come, and she has been using some of our money to finance the building where they live, creating a safe foyer for women and children, with those ladies in charge. All of this, to my surprise. As I said before, baby vampires are not the most empathic creatures in the world.

But not her—not my Mina. She may be a bit more of a psychopath now, but she's still kind. It's surprising, too, how she kept her shifting gift even after becoming a vampire. I may be ancient, but it seems I still have a lot to learn about magical creatures.

We've spent the past few months searching for other shifters, hoping to find her family. It has strangely become her new obsession. Vampires are, unfortunately, stubborn. No luck so far. Either the shifters are exceptionally good at hiding, or they're dead. And if they are alive, they'll have some serious explaining to do about abandoning my Mina when she was a baby.

We flew to Norway for the wedding, like I said we would. Night has fallen—vampire guests would not have appreciated a noon wedding—and its reflection shows on the quiet sea. As promised, our old lands are still untouched by mortals, so we had to bring an entire cargo of mortal men and women to provide enough food for our guests.

Mina stands before me, fabulous, her chest adorned with one of my most recent gifts —a necklace made of diamonds and emeralds, a souvenir of her green eyes. She reaches for my hand, and we both turn toward Josua, our officiant—yes, he has a few jobs.

I see him watching one of Mina's friends—Cherie, I believe—and this one is returning him a charming smile, and I swear I think I heard Josua snort. Something may be happening there.

As he gets back to us, he talks about our vows. I am not listening; instead, I search for Mina's eyes. She turns her face to me, smiling. The naughty smile. The happy smile. She squeezes my hand while looking at me from under her eyelashes, batting them a few times.

I hold back a laugh, and before Josua can pronounce us husband and wife, I grab her, kissing her.

"Fine." Josua sighs. "I now proclaim you husband and wife. Long live the King! Long live the Queen!"

The end.

Pauline Walters is a French author of dark romance and paranormal romance, now living in New Zealand after being trapped by a Kiwi (the man, not the bird.) She enjoys writing stories mostly to get them out of her head, and love strong female leaders who are also showing off their weak side. When she's not writing, she's probably running after her toddler or reading a book.

<u>**Dangerous Double-Jeu**</u>

What do you mean there's another killer in town?

Eve is perfectly content living her double life: office admin champion by day, a calculating serial killer by night. She had it all under control, kind of, until a new predator emerges in Dublin.

Eve can't ignore him. It would be easier if she was not getting distracted by Cyrus McRory, a handsome and sexy-as-hell gang leader.

So what's a girl got to do? Hunt the other killer, of course - while also having a good time.

I'm getting married tonight. I just don't know who my husband is yet.

Emeline Du Bois was raised by vampires, and today is the big day—her wedding day. The only problem? Her parents never told her who she's marrying.

Surprise! Her soon-to-be husband is none other than Romulus—the dangerous, ruthless Alpha of the Broceliande forest, and their mortal enemy.

Marry him. Seduce him. Rule his pack.

That's the plan.

<u>Whispers of the She-Wolf</u>

Angeline Delacour has spent her life walking the thin line between perfection and lies. Cursed with telepathic powers but gifted with a White Wolf twin, Angeline hides her true self from everyone, but especially from herself.

But everything shatters the day she meets **Maros**, one of the **First Vampires** and the most dangerous creature on earth.

Angeline has no time to reflect on their meeting when an incident sends the young woman to the toughest convent in Europe, where years of isolation and torture harden her heart and deepen her mistrust of the world. When war tears her from her confinement, she finds herself a captive in Maros's grip.